IDIOT MEN

short stories

SCOTT GOULD

www.vineleavespress.com

Idiot Men
Copyright © 2023 Scott Gould

All rights reserved.
Print Edition
ISBN: 978-3-98832-030-8
Published by Vine Leaves Press 2023

No parts of this publication may be reproduced, stored in a retrieval system, or transmitted in any form or by any means, electronic, mechanical, photocopying, recording, or otherwise, without the prior written permission of the copyright owner.

This book is sold subject to the condition that it shall not, by way of trade or otherwise, be lent, resold, hired out, or otherwise circulated without the publisher's prior consent in any form of binding or cover other than that in which it is published and without a similar condition including this condition being imposed on the subsequent purchaser. Under no circumstances may any part of this book be photocopied for resale.

This is a work of fiction. Any similarity between the characters and situations within its pages and places or persons, living or dead, is unintentional and coincidental.

Permission has been granted to use excerpts from *Colon Health: The Key to a Vibrant Life*, Dr. N.W. Walker, 1995, Norwalk Press.

Cover design by Jessica Bell
Interior design by Amie McCracken

Praise

"Within the pages of Scott Gould's hilarious and touching *Idiot Men* you'll find a half-broken Chevy Nova, a bald cat, a Smokey the Bear costume, a Naugahyde recliner, a colon-cleaning machine strapped into the bed of an El Camino, six or seven dive bars, a lot of driving, and many many broken hearts. You'll also find a writer able to make you laugh out loud and move you deeply, often in the same sentence. This book is a blast."

NIC BROWN, AUTHOR OF *BANG BANG CRASH*

"Yes, the protagonists in *Idiot Men* make questionable choices at times, but they do so with big-hearted, well-meant, honorable intentions. And if they're idiots, well, they're our idiots. Here's a great congregation of stories, told in Gould's unmistakable voice."

GEORGE SINGLETON, AUTHOR OF
THE CURIOUS LIVES OF NONPROFIT MARTYRS

"Scott Gould is a literary shapeshifter. A rough Southern man who writes about trucks, beer, dogs and doublewides with the finesse of a poet. *Idiot Men* is like the best country song you have ever heard. His writing breaks your heart but makes you rejoice that you are still alive to recover."

JANE STERN, AUTHOR OF *AMBULANCE GIRL*

"'I was built for driving through the night,' says the narrator of 'Word of the Day,' the opening story in *Idiot Men*. Encapsulated here is the thrill of Gould's newest book, which delivers the 'nights' of lost love, cheap booze, and scarred hearts; but also the men who seem destined to 'drive through' the darkness until they seize the dawn. Blending the bloody-knuckled prose of Larry Brown with the black wit of George Singleton, Scott Gould cements his reputation as the South's most unflinching storyteller."
DAN LEACH, AUTHOR OF *DEAD MEDIUMS* AND *FLOODS AND FIRES*

"Scott Gould is the sort of storyteller you'd want sitting next to you on a delayed flight, or (more likely) at a bar. Just when he spins a tale so tall you call for the tab, he tells one that's sobering, and they'll both be on your mind the next morning."
PETER TURCHI, AUTHOR OF
(DON'T) STOP ME IF YOU'VE HEARD THIS BEFORE

"Told in the voices of hapless, hilarious, and sometimes even heroic men, Scott Gould's latest collection offers entertaining portraits and inventive storylines. Sure, these guys are idiots, and they get entangled in some harebrained schemes, but they're also always relatable as they try to overcome broken hearts and jettisoned dreams."
VIRGINIA PYE, AUTHOR OF *THE LITERARY UNDOING OF VICTORIA SWANN* AND *SHELF LIFE OF HAPPINESS*

About the Author

Scott Gould is the author of the five books, including *The Hammerhead Chronicles*, winner of the Eric Hoffer Award for Fiction, and *Things That Crash, Things That Fly*, which won a 2022 Memoir Prize for Books. His other honors include a Next Generation Indie Book Award, an IPPY Award for Fiction, the Larry Brown Short Story Award and the S.C. Arts Commission Artist Fellowship in Prose. His work has appeared in a number of publications, including *Kenyon Review*, *Black Warrior Review*, *Pangyrus*, *New Ohio Review*, *Crazyhorse*, *Pithead Chapel*, *BULL*, *Garden & Gun*, and *New Stories from the South*. He lives in Sans Souci, South Carolina and teaches at the S.C. Governor's School for the Arts & Humanities.

scottgouldwriter.com

*For the full-time men / part-time idiots
who roam the earth.*

Contents

I
Word of the Day - 13
Playing Chicken - 29
The Manila Bond - 51
Taps on the Forehead - 71

II
The Gable Massey Trio
Gable Massey Learns Some Greek - 103
What Gable Massey Did After His Wife Left Him - 133
Gable Massey Makes a Movie - 147

III
Oxygen - 179
The Prince - 201
Smokey the Bear Has the Matches - 229
The Smells at Certain Heights - 255

Acknowledgements - 277

I

Word of the Day

Back when I was first on the road, we used to play this game we called Independent Trucker. I didn't name it. Brandy did that. She's one of those people who likes her words. I'd drive the rig down the interstate to Ollie's and run it through the giant washer. Then, I'd top off both tanks, buy one of those pine sap smelly things hanging from the display near the cash register, and tie it up in the back of the sleeper cab. Sometimes, I'd spring for a new cassette if they had a sale bin, maybe some Billy Joe Royal. By the time I eased out of Ollie's, Brandy would be standing in the emergency lane of I-85, her Honda Accord pulled over in the tall grass with the hood up and a bandana tied to the outside mirror. She'd hear me a half mile away, downshifting and double-clutching for the incline. I liked coming over the rise and catching another gear, accelerating right by her like she was tied to the dock. Then, I'd stand on the air brakes and lose six months of tread.

Brandy was good at playing the game. She never rushed things. She'd wait for the funk of burned rubber to blow away. She always looked like she was weighing her options, standing there in her flowery dress and her hair in that high ponytail. I'd swing the passenger door of the truck open like an invitation, and up she'd climb. We'd drive a half dozen miles to the rest stop near Exit 34, park the truck in one of the long, diagonal spots reserved for long-haulers, and that's where we'd go at each other like scared prom dates a half hour from curfew.

That was back a ways. Back before Brandy brought home that bald cat, back when I was gone five of every seven nights, on I-95 from Jacksonville to Baltimore or dodging weigh stations all the way to the end of I-10 in LA. Fact of the matter, I really *was* an independent trucker, so I didn't have a company writing me mileage checks every couple of weeks. I never drove the same routes twice in a row. I drove wherever somebody paid me for miles, most of the time in envelopes of cash. The years I was running that hard, I was skinny as Barney Fife and could go without sleep for days at a time. I was built for driving through the night.

And Brandy told me early on *she* was built for being married to a man who drove through the night, and I believe she held tight and fast to that thought until the nights started linking together, one right after the other and no end in sight. I still remember some of those arguments when the whole thing started turning sour. Brandy wasn't much of a debater. NASA wasn't putting out a missing person's report for her. She wanted to be smart, but she just wasn't up to the task, especially when we started going at it. (And by going at it, I don't mean the way we used to in the sleeper cab). One time, she got so flustered arguing with me, she went out the next day and bought a little Word-A-Day desk calendar. Brandy convinced herself an expanding vocabulary would strike a match somewhere up in her brain.

Seems every time I came back from a long haul we'd have a long fight. She would block me in the hallway and start demanding to know which highways I'd been up and down. She'd lean in close to try and catch a whiff of my bad intentions. Brandy was as thin as me and almost as tall. We even stalked each other the same way, there in the hall, a couple of shadows dancing around each other.

"How can you be gone that long and not let me know where you were? You're so freaking ubiquitous!" she said one night.

"Freaking what?" I said, and she waved her hand at me.

"If I've got to explain ubiquitous, then that's basically symbiotic of my living hell," she said and stomped off to the bedroom. I lay down on the front couch and closed my eyes for the first good time in half a week. After a decent argument, I could sleep for twelve hours straight.

If Brandy had ever taken the time to see what knick-knacks I brought her from the road, she'd have known where I'd been. Half an oyster shell from the Chesapeake

Bay. A handful of red dirt from the Four Corners stuffed into a plastic sandwich bag. An eagle feather that got sucked into my truck's grill somewhere near Boulder. A piece of bleached-out driftwood from the marsh outside Savannah. And on and on. Little souvenirs of my geography. I got no idea what she did with all those tiny mementos.

Maybe she gave them to Miss Dana. Miss Dana, down the road a half mile, in a vinyl-sided house with a wide porch wrapped around three sides of it. Brandy liked to go over there, and the two of them would sit on the side of the house nearest the sun and drink piña coladas and pretend they were somewhere else. I'm not making this up. Brandy told me once, when we were arguing and playing chicken in the hallway, "At least I got a place to matriculate and drink something that tastes like coconuts and imagine not cohabitating with you."

?

You could fill up a tractor trailer with the things I don't understand because I just don't give a shit. But the things I'll never understand because I don't have the brain for it? They would fit in a smaller space. For instance, I'll never figure out why Brandy adopted that bald cat. She named it Princess Di because she picked out the cat the very same Sunday she heard that the Princess had come to her end during that car chase over in Paris. "She was so…so damn somnambulant. I actually cried," Brandy told me when she walked in with a little plastic pet carrier.

Brandy didn't say right off her new cat was one of those strange and rare breeds that don't possess a shred of fur. But when that animal sashayed out of the carrier, I thought the thing had been parboiled or just come from chemotherapy. All Brandy said was, "Eddie, this is Princess Di," and I'm no cat expert, but I could tell from a distance that thing wasn't any princess, what with that pair of hairless, aspirin-size balls waggling between his back legs. From where I stood, he was more rodent than cat. But Brandy loved Princess Di and took him everywhere: to the store, to visit Dana, to get her hair done. Princess Di was comfortable on a leash, and he would lead Brandy down the sidewalk in front of the house. When he wasn't strutting down the street, Princess Di weaved through rooms, rubbing up against furniture, looking like he was making evil cat plans he would carry out when we weren't watching.

?

Some folks might say the bald cat was the thing that pushed us over the edge, but I think the two of us—me and Brandy—just reached a point of mutual surrender. In trucker terms, you could say we both got way out of range and couldn't seem to pick each other up on the CB anymore. Brandy didn't agree, at least I don't think she did. She pulled out one of her words and said we had become severely *dilated*. "Dilated to the point that I need to get the hell out of town," she said. I couldn't imagine Brandy out in the world on her own, but she sat down at the kitchen table and called a travel agent she found in the yellow pages. She wasn't going alone either. "Dana really wants to supplicate piña coladas beneath an honest-to-god palm tree, so she's going with me." As if I didn't have enough to filter through my brain at that particular moment, Brandy said, "Please plan to be off the road the weekend we're gone. I can't leave the cat alone. Princess Di will shred everything out of salubrious loneliness and depression."

From all my nights on the highway, I knew a little about lonely, and, for a split second, I felt sorry for Princess Di. Then he walked in the room, and I took in all of his hairless rodentness. I wasn't sure I could stomach taking care of something so embarrassing looking. But the last thing I wanted was more trouble, so I promised to leave the truck under the metal carport for a few days. I thought to myself, *A little space might be good for all of us.* "I could do some yard work," I said.

"That would be insouciant," Brandy answered me right back, and, like most times, I had no idea what she said or, for that matter, where I stood.

?

I know how it is with the little things in the world. I've run eighty-thousand pounds of semi eighty miles an hour down an arrow-straight highway in West Texas in the middle of the night and hit a fence nail the size of a thimble. Next thing I know, I've shredded an inside rear, and I'm stuck on the shoulder until dawn. The big things, you can usually see them coming. But those little things are always the surprise. In my mind, the fact the pantry was all but empty was a little thing. I opened it up the morning after Brandy and Miss Dana left in Brandy's Honda for the airport in Charlotte. I didn't figure I could live on a can of tuna fish and baking potatoes that were sprouting from the eyes. Princess Di had more food than I did. I needed a grocery trip.

I was all set to run down to the Stop-N-Go when I noticed the stack of Food Lion coupons behind a refrigerator magnet. Not the most convenient grocery store to the house, but it was hard to bypass double savings. I grabbed my wallet, my ring of keys, and the coupons and was almost through the door when I remembered what Brandy had said about Princess Di's behavior when left on his own. I decided locking him in the hall closet for an hour while I was at the Food Lion would not cause him any stress. I thought, *He won't lose any hair over it*, and laughed out loud.

I idled the rig at the far end of the Food Lion lot, grabbed a cart outside, and almost knocked Dana over at the automatic door. *Maybe this is still a little thing*, I thought. Dana looked over my shoulder, like I was blocking her view of a sunset she didn't want to miss. I couldn't think of a thing to say, and the only noise was the automatic door buzzing and clicking because it couldn't decide exactly what to do. The door wasn't the only thing confused right about then, but I came back to my senses and said, "This don't look much like Jamaica to me, Miss Dana."

Dana dropped the bag she was holding, and most of her shopping trip fell out. A bottle of piña colada mix banged to a stop under a gumball machine. "I'm visiting my mother," she said when she bent to pick up the things under her feet. She machine-gunned words at me. "She's sick. I had to get groceries. It's an emergency. Plans changed. That's all." I didn't move. I drive a truck. I'm used to backing up traffic. People with carts full of grocery bags lined up behind Dana. I saw her start to wilt. She didn't know which way to go. I could tell she wanted to walk over to the gumball machine and grab her piña colada mix. "I had to cancel our trip at the last minute. My mother. She's not well, like I said. Plans changed."

Me, I was trying to put it all together, trying to think of some good and decent reason why Dana was in the Food Lion and my wife was in Jamaica. "Is Brandy back at your house?" I asked her because I thought, *Well, maybe they made their own little getaway on Dana's sunny porch.*

Dana hugged her groceries to her chest. "No, Eddie. She's not with me." When I didn't say anything, she kept on. "She's gone to Jamaica."

"Well, okay then," I said. "The question left here between you and me is why she went to Jamaica all by herself. Did she need a vacation that bad? To go all on her own?"

Dana cocked her head like a curious dog. I let what I'd asked her hang in the air for a moment.

"Or," I said, "the question could be, who she's down there with?" Dana didn't say a word. "The way questions work, Dana, is that I ask one and you get to answer it," I said.

Behind us, in the line of stalled grocery carts, a guy said something about taking our conversation somewhere else, and I shot him a look that could singe hair from a distance.

"I got no answer," Dana said. "I don't like being caught in the middle." She started to walk by me, but, skinny as I was, I still filled up too much of the door.

"Well, you're definitely caught there. Who is it?" I said.

Dana shifted gears. "Why is it you men always ask that? You think it's going to make you feel any better?"

I was closest to the gumball machine, so I reached under there for her pina colada mix. I handed it to Dana. "Well, the more you know, the more you know," I said, and I couldn't begin to tell you why. Maybe I wanted to sound clever, like a television commercial or something.

"You won't feel better," she said. Beyond Miss Dana and the folks leaning on their shopping carts, I saw a manager-looking fellow wearing a tie walking fast our way.

"Who?" I asked again.

"God, think about it, connect some dots," Dana said, and I let her brush by me into the parking lot.

?

To be honest, that was one of my better qualities: being able to think through a situation. Driving twelve, fourteen hours at a crack for years on end had put my brain into a permanent low gear. I always thought things through to their logical conclusions. And that was why I didn't react too badly when Dana told me Brandy was on a three-day, all-inclusive Jamaican package. She just wouldn't tell me with who.

But she was right. I needed to think about this, and I always thought best when I was on the road, so I drove out to Ollie's, put two hundred dollars worth of diesel in the rig, and went north on 85. Sixty miles down the road, I still had no real answers, but I did happen to recall I'd left a bald cat cooped up in my hall closet.

I have to say, I've always hated backtracking, especially early in a trip. Retracing the miles I'd just rolled onto the odometer made me feel like a failure. But I thought it through. If I kept on going north on 85, just kept going and going, the cat would eventually stink up the closet, probably the whole house, maybe even die, which would leave me with cleaning up and explaining to do. (I had to laugh at the fact that I might be the one with explaining to do after Brandy's Jamaican trip.)

It took a couple of miles of head-scratching, but I decided to go back for Princess Di. The possible ends weren't worth all the means. Starving to death was no way for any creature to come to an end, even an ugly ass cat. I didn't consider myself a cruel man, and, at this point, the thought of what to do with the cat hadn't crossed my mind yet. That came later.

On the way back for Princess Di, I couldn't help but wonder about every trip I ever took and what Brandy had been up to while I watched the front of the truck eat up hundreds of thousands of white dashes in the asphalt. I replayed all the times I called home, turning up the volume on my cell phone to be able to hear Brandy over the rumble of the engine, but ending up leaving voice messages because she was always out. Or the time I pulled in a couple of days early and she was gone—on a last-minute overnight trip with Dana to Atlanta. I knew it wasn't healthy sifting through the past on the lookout for lies. Like I said, I hated backtracking.

Princess Di was one pissed-off cat when I got home. He made a beeline to the litter box and camped out there for a few minutes. He watched me load up a used grocery bag full of his food, his bowl (the one Brandy made for him at Clay Creations), and his little pillow. Like most animals I had ever come across, Princess Di was mostly attached to people and food, which was why he didn't seem to complain when I tossed him in the back corner of the sleeper cab.

By the time the truck hit seventy, I was talking to Princess Di, which I have to say was a comfort—the fact that I had something listening to me that wouldn't be able to talk back. I'd turn my chin a little over my shoulder and holler back toward the sleeper cab, "You ever heard of Jamaica, Princess Di? It's an island where people go with their boyfriends and work on their vocabulary," or "I got me a couple of words of the day for your momma, Princess Di," or I'd say, "Brandy is probably floating in a pool near a beach, drinking something frozen with two straws in it, and on one end of one of those straws is a man who doesn't drive a truck."

I squinted through the windshield, trying hard to see who was sucking on that straw. I asked Princess Di if he had any ideas. "You probably know exactly who the hell it is," I said out loud. "Probably watched them doing it."

I don't know why, but I started aiming whatever I was feeling in the wrong direction and found myself getting pissed at the bald cat. I could wait a couple of hours, then toss him from the truck on the lonely section of the interstate between Raleigh and South Hill. I could almost drive that section asleep and honestly had come close to doing just that many a time. It was straight and uninteresting, with long stretches where you could see a couple of miles down the road in either direction. I could grab Princess Di and backhand him through the open window. At seventy miles an hour, a hairless cat would explode on impact.

"You can save yourself if you tell me who your momma's with. Turn into a talking cat, and I'll pull you off of death row," I said. I angled the mirror toward the sleeper cab. Princess Di purred at me, and, for a second, I thought he might actually have something to say about the whole situation.

I was pretty familiar with myself. I knew the not-knowing was going to eat me up. Ever since I was a kid, I'd go nuts if somebody kept a secret from me. And I was sure Miss Dana wouldn't tell. She had her chance at the Food Lion. The bald cat wasn't yakking up any information either. When I left the house, I forgot to grab the piece of paper with an 800 number for Brandy's hotel in Jamaica. "Only for emergencies," she'd said on her way out the door. "You can leave me and Dana a message at the front desk. Cell phones are inscrutable in Jamaica. That's what the brochure says."

So I was just driving. Just pointing the truck and running through the gears, being careful like always not to grind anything. I didn't have a plan in mind until I got a sign. An omen out of the blue. I swear, it might as well have been the hand of God hitting the air brakes and downshifting when I saw the sign for the Charlotte airport. I don't think I was in charge of anything at that point—destiny, the clutch, whatever. It just happened. I rolled up the exit ramp.

In the split second it took me to read the exit sign, I realized what I had to do with Princess Di, what to do about Brandy, what to do about the answers I didn't have for the questions I'd been asking myself the last ninety miles.

I parked the truck in the emergency lane of the access road that led to all of the long-term parking lots at the Charlotte airport. I didn't know how many of those lots they have (still don't), but I guessed about a half dozen or so. I had plenty of time. I put the leash around Princess Di's hairless little neck and set off on foot with the cat. I can imagine what we looked like. Skinny fellow in Tony Lama boots, walking a bald cat on a leash. Folks stared from their cars, and I can't blame them.

I'd duck under the gate of each lot and walk up and down the rows of cars. On my big ring, I had an extra key fob thing for Brandy's Accord, so I pointed it in all directions and pushed the little button on the top. I was hoping to hear that chirp when I got within range of the Honda. I didn't have any luck in the first lot—or the second or even the third. By the time I hit number four, I was carrying Princess Di under my arm like a loaf of bread. He'd had enough asphalt for the day. I pushed the button on the Honda key and there in the distance, I heard the car answer back. Pushed again and there was the sound.

All I had to do was follow my ears until I saw that little Accord, its horn squeaking and its headlights flashing every time I pushed the button. I think even Princess Di recognized the car because he started squirming under my elbow. I put him down and let him walk the rest of the way. When he reached the car, he rubbed against its tires and sniffed the rocker panel.

I didn't come to the long-term lot unprepared. I had that bag of food and that bowl I could fill up from a water bottle. Had that little pillow too. I laid the food and water on the floorboard on the passenger's side. I cracked all the windows a couple of inches. This was the beginning of November. That bald cat wasn't going to roast. Princess Di drank about half a bowl of water while I spread food on the floor mat. I refilled the bowl and shut the doors. Princess Di looked up at me and meowed. "She'll be back in two days. You'll survive, so shut up," I said through the glass. "In fact, you damn well better survive, you bald bastard. I want you nice and regular for a couple of days." Then, I backtracked to my rig and headed south on the interstate, headed for home. I missed having Princess Di in the sleeper cab, but I didn't even think about going back for him. I was not hauling regrets with me.

?

Counting the afternoon I left that bald cat in the parking lot, there were exactly fifty-four days left in the year. Which means there were fifty-four vocabulary words left on Brandy's Word-A-Day desk calendar. I made fifty-four phone calls to some front desk clerk in Jamaica who kept forwarding me to a voicemail line for a Ms. Brandy Hollingsworth. And every time I got on that voicemail, I left a message containing the word of the day. Fifty-four messages, each one with a strange word. I got to admit, I tried to understand the definitions and use the words correctly, but I felt like Brandy, stumbling around with the language. At least I knew I was messing up. I told her she had totaled my sangfroid. I said that there would be an antepenultimate waiting for her in the parking lot. I called her a gribble. I didn't care if I made any sense.

Turns out, Brandy never set foot in our house again. I wished she had, so she could tell me what her Honda Accord smelled like when she and her traveling companion returned from Jamaica, all tanned and worn out and ready to get home. To this day, I can't tell you who the man was. But I can tell you that Princess Di survived his short vacation in the Accord. I heard from Miss Dana that the bald cat is alive but very wary of floorboards of any kind.

If Brandy ever does come back, I've got a little something for her from the road, a little souvenir from my trip to the Charlotte airport. Still have it stuck to the refrigerator, right where the Food Lion coupons used to be. It's a parking receipt, the one I took off Brandy's dash when I left that bald cat in the long-term parking. Has the time and date when she left for Jamaica stamped right on it.

I don't know why I took it. I'll bet there's a word for that.

Playing Chicken

I am a home health nurse for Williamsburg County. My present occupation has not caused me to be shot at, molested, or otherwise screwed with because I am six feet, four inches tall and weigh two hundred and sixty-five pounds and have an attitude that repels ridicule like the back side of a magnet. The last time someone attempted humor in regard to me being a male nurse, I broke his nose. Then, I set it for him. I am a nurse because it required very little money and effort to get into tech school classes when I took leave of Parris Island, a garden spot where I lost both of my big toenails and sixteen pounds while I learned to be a Marine war machine.

That is all to say that between then and now, I have put many a mile on my Plymouth Valiant, negotiating the swampy two-ruts of this county where people have more concern for the lotto numbers than their health. I have calculated the blood pressure of people who exist two ticks from a heart attack. I have listened to the sloshing lungs of those who smell like the insides of an ashtray. And I have wedged medicine spoons between the brown teeth of squirming, squealing children. Through it all, I have come to believe that the human body is nothing more than a private trash heap some of us fill to capacity faster than others.

Yet I do not come to preach. I come today with a message, and it is this: Folks you wouldn't normally put together are winding up under the same roof. And they are getting along.

Not only are they getting along, they are growing intimately familiar and consequently having babies, crisscrossing boundaries like smugglers with a bag of dope and a bad sense of direction. It is perhaps a health situation to monitor.

Think about this:

Some months ago, I pulled the Valiant onto a road that paralleled a set of railroad tracks. Behind me, the tracks ran toward a pair of hills, where they disappeared into a curve of green trees growing so close to the tracks, the limbs were shaved and bare on one side from the constant scrape of freight cars. In front of me, the tracks eventually pulled up behind the Victoria Chicken Plant, where the slogan is right there, in big letters across the front of the building: *We Are Why The Chickens Cross The Road*.

During shift changes, groups of Hispanic men, wearing black hip boots and long white coats, walk between the plant and any number of trailer parks tucked in the trees along the tracks. I have an EMT buddy who gets summoned to the chicken plant once or twice a month when a line worker loses a finger to a bone saw or slips and bangs his head and nearly drowns in the chicken goop coating the floor. He says walking into the chicken plant is a stroll straight through the gates of Hell. He told me once that there isn't enough money in the world to make him spend a shift in the chicken plant, and I told him he hadn't been poor enough yet. I would work there before I'd starve. I just wouldn't eat chicken tenders anymore. I would adapt.

I was searching for a trailer park called—swear to God—Camelot. Lot number sixty-five. My patient notes said that a Chevy Nova would be parked outside the trailer. I never saw an official Camelot sign, just rode through little clusters of mud-stained trailers until I ultimately turned into a gravel driveway and spotted the Nova. It was bright yellow with a back end jacked up in the direction of ten o'clock. It appeared some sort of unwashed animal had expired on the front dash, the clay-colored fur matted against the window. Enough religious icons to save a small town from holy terror dangled from the rearview mirror along with a silvery CD. The car was running, leaking gray smoke, not from where the exhaust pipe should be, but from some hole in the undercarriage. The engine noise reminded me of hearts I had heard through my stethoscope, those on the near side of complete breakdown. Somebody was warming up the car, getting ready to leave.

I knocked on the door and heard the growl rise from under the steps. I knew there would be a dog. There's *always* a dog. Dogs come as standard equipment at my patients' homes. Alarm systems on four legs. Cheap and mean and won't quit when the power goes out. I'm never unprepared. I simply bent and put my head close to the top step. And I growled back. In five years, there hasn't been a dog that returned my call of the wild.

I felt in my front pocket for the little card of health-related Spanish sayings. I used this cheat sheet to get through visits in the area around the chicken plant. With my laminated card, I could say things like "Where does it hurt?" and "When was the last time you went to the bathroom?" and "You'd better see a doctor before you drop dead of a heart attack." Most of the chicken plant people spoke more English than I could Spanish. We always worked out our communication problems one way or the other.

The door opened, and the way the sun hit the screen door, I couldn't see anything or anyone through the sudden glare. "Hola," I said to a thin silhouette that appeared in the open space.

"You from the department?" a woman asked back.

When I said yes, the screen door opened, and I walked into the most amazing shrine to NASCAR I had ever seen in my life. In a single quick glance, I couldn't pick out this fan's particular favorite. They seemed to love anybody who drove. Photos of cars spread across the walls. Trinkets covered the counters: NASCAR keychains, NASCAR money clips, NASCAR fork and spoon sets, NASCAR pocket knives, NASCAR playing cards, NASCAR lip balm. The trailer smelled like the inside of a Waffle House—bacon and coffee and cigarette smoke.

"Sit down anywhere," she told me. My eyes adjusted to the dimmer light. She was far from Hispanic. She was thin and redheaded. The mere thought of going outside would probably raise a sunburn on her. I suspected she might be a little bit anemic, and I had to remind myself I wasn't here to see her. I was here about a baby.

"You speak English," I said and smiled.

"Course I do. I'm English."

"I'm sorry," I said. "I was expecting someone Hispanic."

"And I was expecting a nurse," she said. "My name is Gonzales. Wanda Gonzales. I need somebody to take a look at Ho-el."

"Ho-el?"

"He's in the back bedroom." Wanda left me standing alone in the NASCAR museum.

I spent the next dozen seconds or so wondering what the name Ho-el could be short for. Maybe he had an attitude. Holy Hell. Ho-el. It was a nickname I had never heard before. She came back holding a redheaded kid with his face buried in her Earnhardt t-shirt. He finally peeked out, and I could see how brown his eyes were. My notes said he was three years old, and this kid looked about that age. She sat down with her boy.

"Here's the card about the shots he's done had," she said, pushing a piece of paper across the table at my knees. At the sound of the word *shots*, Ho-el buried his head deeper into the face of Dale Earnhardt. I read the card to myself. *Joel Gonzales.* J-O-E-L.

"So your husband calls him Ho-el."

"My husband don't call him nothing. My husband don't call, period."

I tried a communication trick I learned in a seminar the county paid for. I paused and didn't say a word. Wanda grew uncomfortable with the lack of talking, just like I hoped.

"He's gone. Been gone. He used to call him Ho-el. That's the Mexican way to say it, I suppose."

"So that's not your husband's car outside?" I looked around for a boyfriend hiding behind a door.

"That's mine. '75 Nova. Stock."

"Well, your car is running, ma'am."

"I can't turn it off," she said.

I went silent again. I was having trouble with this conversation.

"Ho-el broke off the key in the ignition a couple weeks ago. I don't know how to hotwire it, so I just keep putting gas in. I even changed the oil while it was running once. You try that sometime. I don't know what the hell I'm gonna do if a belt breaks." She was proud of herself. I looked at Ho-el. Three years old and he already had grease under his tiny little fingernails. I saw his future. He would know how to change a water pump before he could read.

"What's wrong with Ho-el?" I leaned forward.

"He's been punk lately." She pushed the red hair away from Ho-el's forehead. He did look pale, but, then again, his momma was almost see-through.

"Punk?"

"Kinda down in the dumps. He ain't happy like he usually is. He's usually all over the place, tearing things up. He's a little stemwinder most of the time. This here ain't the normal everyday Ho-el."

I asked her to let me take a look at him, but Ho-el had a death grip on his momma and Dale Earnhardt. She pried him off like a scared kitten and handed him across the table.

Ho-el weighed next to nothing, as if he was filled with warm air. His eyes were big and scared, and because they were opened wide, I could see they oozed more than tears. I managed one quick feel of the glands in his throat, which were about the size of hickory nuts. When I touched an ear, he let out a yell.

"Well, Ho-el's definitely sick," I said.

"No shit," she said, rummaging through the papers on the table for a cigarette lighter.

"I'm going to give you some antibiotic samples. They should be enough to get him well. If you need more, call the Health Department." I pulled a double handful of samples from my bag. "Can he take pills?"

"He'll swallow anything with chocolate on it. Say thank you, Ho-el," she said.

"Gracias," he whispered in a raspy little voice.

Ho-el's momma stood up. "I'll give you a ride back into town," she said.

Wanda was making a habit of confusing me. "But I drove my car."

"Yeah, but you ain't got but a couple of wheels left on it." Outside, the Valiant listed awkwardly to the left like a wounded animal. I hadn't heard a sound when my wheels were stolen. I'd been so intent on Ho-el and his momma.

For a second, I found it difficult to breathe. I completely forgot about a child being in the room. "Goddamn chicken workers," I said. It was at that point that Ho-el's momma clipped my jaw with the quickest right cross I'd ever made contact with. I was too impressed with the way she cut her punch to be angry. I smacked the table to keep my balance.

"You watch that mouth of yours," she said. "I don't care if you are from the county, that's not a nice thing to say." The dog under the step must have heard the commotion. He came sort of running from the back of the trailer, where I suppose he had a doggie door, a *tiny* doggie door because he was a Chihuahua no bigger than an average-sized ham. His growl made him seem exponentially larger. He must have picked up that whole sound-bigger-than-you-really-are routine from having to defend himself against the larger mongrels and curs of the world.

"Surprises me that someone like you would say such things about folks," she said. Maybe she thought the fact I was a male nurse automatically put a bull's eye on my back for abuse, that I was oppressed. Whatever she meant, I didn't care because I was watching her dog try and make his way toward me. It appeared he couldn't go straight. To get from point A to B, he spun in little circles, one right after another, a tiny short-haired cyclone.

"Your dog can't walk a straight line," I said, feeling fortunate that my jaw still worked. Being a nurse, I knew what a pain in the ass a broken jaw could be.

"Horgay hit him in the head with a golf club one afternoon, and he's been turning circles ever since. It takes him half an hour to get from one end of the yard to the other. Mostly, he sleeps under the trailer. He's not a bad watchdog." She thought about that for a second. "Until he has to chase something," she added. "Hey, you want to buy anything before you go?" She waved her arm over the room. It was at that moment I noticed each item in this particular NASCAR shrine had a tiny price tag.

"Oh, I see. You sell things."

She said, "I got to make ends meet somehow. Horgay got tired of wading through chicken guts and left us to go back to Juarez. He said he'd send money. Ain't that some shit? Going *back* to Mexico to make money. Let's just say, I ain't holding my breath for the mailman to deliver a shoebox full of damn pesos, so I buy all this stuff from a guy in a step-van, double the price, and sell it to the neighbors. Listen bud, Mexicans love car racing. Good god, if there was a Mexican driving at Daytona, they couldn't sell enough tickets. I make more farting around doing this than Horgay ever brought home shucking feathers off hens."

At the mention of Horgay, I thought I saw little Ho-el tear up. Then, he sneezed and I knew the watery eyes were because of his cold or his allergies or whatever sort of ailment he had in his head and throat.

"I'll just walk. It isn't that far," I said. "He doesn't need to be going out, anyway. I'll send somebody to tow the car tomorrow. Just don't let them take anything else off it, okay?" The dog had finally made his way to me and was trying to figure out if my shoe—size fourteen—was worth humping on. He turned a few circles around my leg, then left me alone, not agreeing with my smell or my attitude. Little Ho-el was already asleep on the couch, whistling through his half-clogged nose.

"I might be able to get your wheels back. I think I know who it is that's got them," she offered. I handed her my card just in case.

I checked the Valiant. The spare was still in the trunk, so I was only one wheel short. I started along the railroad tracks toward the Victoria Chicken Plant, checking my watch to make sure a shift change wasn't about to come marching in my direction. As it turned out, I was the only one walking the rails that hour. The smell from the plant gave me a headache, and I wondered if maybe little Ho-el was allergic to chicken fumes when the wind blew in the wrong direction.

Idiot Men

?

I do not believe in fate. I do not believe in love or faith. I do not believe in any of life's abstractions. Which is why I do not believe there was any hidden meaning in the fact I happened to return to Ho-el's trailer the next morning, a Saturday morning, at *precisely* ten o'clock. I wasn't attracted to the trailer like a homing pigeon. I was not relishing another encounter with the sidewinder dog. I simply wanted my damn car back. I hated being without transportation and at the mercy of my sore feet.

I took a smelly taxicab back to Camelot. Along with me, I carried a used rim and tire I bought for twenty-five bucks. When I pulled up to the trailer, I immediately knew that things were different. For one, the Nova was sitting quiet. For another, the Valiant was gone. And that little hurricane of a dog was sleeping on the top step, not hiding beneath it. He didn't twitch a muscle when I climbed the steps. For a second, I thought he was dead. He moved slightly when the cab pulled away.

Nobody answered my knock on the door, which opened easily when I pushed on it. The little dog cocked open one eye and sighed, like he already knew it wasn't worth going in. I hadn't walked three steps across the room when I heard an entire fleet of cars screech into the yard—three sheriff's department cruisers with the lights flashing and the headlights blinking. No sirens. The ten o'clock sneak attack.

"You in there, come on out, right now," a man called through a bullhorn, his voice loud and cracking a little like he was nervous.

I walked onto the top step, forgetting about the dog, which I nudged in the ribs purely by accident. He growled at me, and I don't blame him. Deputies crouched behind their open car doors.

"Sir, you are not from around here." His surprise was amplified by the bullhorn.

"I'm from the Health Department," I said, reaching into my pocket for my official ID card. I thought it might work like a badge, making us brothers-in-public-service or some such.

"Whoa now, watch that hand there, chief," he said. The men hiding behind their police cruisers all flinched a bit.

"I'm a nurse with the Health Department. I'm trying to find my car. I saw a sick little boy right here yesterday." He walked toward me. A good sign. He quit using the bullhorn.

"A nurse? You shitting me. You know anything about counterfeit NASCAR paraphernalia?" he asked me.

"Counterfeit?" I asked back, ignoring his high-pitched reaction to my being a nurse.

"Bet your ass."

"Counterfeit how? How do you know?" I said.

He raised one eyebrow. "I get paid to know, buddy," he said, nodding, drawing me into a kind of awkward confidence with him.

It took him and his deputies a half an hour to scrape all the NASCAR things into boxes and load them into the back of a couple of patrol cars. They could have gone faster if they hadn't stopped to admire all of the different trinkets. I started to tell them I thought my car was stolen, but I wasn't really sure that was the case. It could have been simply borrowed. It struck me that I was protecting Ho-el's momma for a reason I couldn't put my finger on. Running a counterfeit NASCAR ring out of a trailer—that was impressive. Her frailness was a disguise. That was impressive, too.

"Listen, you want to do me a favor? You hear from this guy, you let us know. We can't have him selling fake NASCAR stuff, even if it is to other Mexicans," he told me.

So he didn't know about Ho-el's momma. They obviously thought it was Horgay doing the selling. I let out some breath, realizing that she wasn't going to be arrested. The relief surprised me.

I told him I'd keep an eye out, and suddenly, it was just me and the dog and the trailer. With the merchandise gone, an echoing emptiness filled the rooms. "I suppose I'm walking again," I said to the dog, and he must have been bilingual because he followed on my heels, whirling his dervishes between the railroad tracks. I had to go slow, what with the dog and the tire I rolled along. I was beginning to feel stupid and careless, and those feelings never lead anywhere good.

?

That night, in my tiny rental house, I evaluated what I had and what I didn't. I didn't have a car at the moment. That situation needed a solution immediately. I was intelligent enough to know I should call that sheriff and report it stolen. But there were holes in my intel. And a call to the sheriff might implicate Ho-el and his mother in some way. *There you go again, acting like a nurse*, I thought, *taking care of people you don't really know.* I had a spare tire on my kitchen table. I had a dizzy Chihuahua on my kitchen floor. I had been feeding him boiled peanuts all afternoon, and he'd become exceedingly gassy. I'd shell a handful of the soggy peanuts, he'd eat them, raise himself up, then turn a couple of circles and leave a vapor trail behind him, which, of course, he kept spinning into. You wouldn't automatically assume something so small could conjure up an odor so foul. I began to feel sorry for a creature that kept revolving into his own biological functions.

We both fell asleep just after dark, me upright in the kitchen chair and the Chihuahua wrapped around as much of my feet as he could cover. The machine gun blasts of a straight-piped exhaust in my driveway woke us both. The dog growled at the noise. I felt him rumble against my leg. He was a fearless little dog. Outside, two men sprinted away in the darkness, their footsteps slapping the pavement. What they left behind was my Valiant, but it wasn't the same. It had been modified. It was jacked up in the back. Strips of white shag carpet ringed every window. A Virgin Mary dangled from the mirror. A note fluttered under the windshield wiper. It said: *I told them to fix up your car or I would turn them in.* The meaning of "fix up" must have been lost in translation. But Wanda was looking out for me and my Valiant. It had been a long time since someone had thought about me.

That night, the dog and I rode out to Camelot in the loud, renovated Valiant. When we got there, the windows in the trailer were dark and someone had removed the front door. The dog refused to get out of the car, as if to say he wasn't interested in making a dramatic reentrance. I stuck my head into the darkness and smelled it right off. Somebody had deliberately made the worst kinds of messes inside, bathroom types of things. It wasn't healthy.

So, that was that. This trailer was not going to be fit for man or beast for a long time. Life goes on and all that.

"Screw them," I said. No more Wanda, no more Ho-El. I said it, but my heart wasn't really in it.

Inside the Valiant, the dog raised his head at me. "I'm gonna call you Roundabout," I said, and I turned the key, blowing smoke and making noise enough to wake the dead.

?

But it wasn't the end of things. A couple of months later, I pulled up to the Health Department in the same old Valiant. I had tried to sell it, but nobody wanted to pay my firm asking price. No one wanted a car that looked like a carnival-ride reject. It took me a while, but I finally realized the reason I wouldn't budge on the price: I really wanted to keep the Valiant. I had grown accustomed to the bark of the pipes and the clouds of exhaust that barely disguised the glares from folks at stoplights. I didn't care. I had a loud car that cranked every time I turned the key and a dog curled on the front seat that appreciated Motown. Roundabout went on all my calls with me, guarding the Valiant. I didn't know dogs liked music, much less did I know that a Chihuahua would enjoy, say, Martha and the Vandellas.

I left Roundabout on the front seat and walked in to sort through my schedule of patients for the morning. The receptionist, a sleepy-eyed woman who herded the sick all day long from the protection of her desk, told me a man was waiting in the lobby. "He's Hispanic," she whispered like some sort of storm warning.

The man was watching the television blaring in the waiting room, hypnotized, as if it was the first time he had ever seen one. When I approached him, he didn't get up from the chair, just kept glancing at the game show on channel twelve.

"Buenos dias," he said. "You have my dog."

"Excuse me?" I said, which is what I usually say when I'm caught off guard.

"I'm Jorge Gonzales and you have my Chihuahua. Someone saw you in your Plymouth near the plant with Diablo. My dog, Diablo. The devil dog."

"I thought you went back to Mexico," I answered.

"I have returned."

"Well, yes," I said slowly, editing as I spoke. "I have *a* dog. I'm not sure it's *your* dog."

"This dog, my dog, is a dog of many spirals. I golfed him once." Horgay finally rose. He was small and doughy. His eyes didn't match the rest of him. They were very confident. But his body didn't look like it could back up any kind of threat his eyes laid down. "I thank you very much for taking care of Diablo. I will have him back now."

"I don't have him here." I lied.

Horgay began tapping his pockets. "Something to write?" he asked. He left me his address and telephone number. "You can bring him by, yes?"

"I suppose," I answered. "If it's yours, of course."

"Ho-el needs a pet," he said, and, dammit, that ruined it for me. I remembered Ho-el's runny eyes and wheezy cough. Yes, a boy like that could use an animal in his life.

"Yeah, I'll bring him," I told him. "This afternoon, after work." Horgay nodded and sat down to finish watching his game show.

?

The address Horgay gave me was another trailer park, not far from Camelot. I snatched up Roundabout and carried him under my arm to the door. He passed a little gas when I squeezed him. *Good*, I thought. I'd fed him about a quarter pound of boiled peanuts that afternoon for his return to Horgay. I wanted him to make an impressive entrance.

The Nova was nowhere to be seen. Instead, an old Monte Carlo sat in the short driveway, its quarter panel rusting, the trunk tied shut with a piece of copper wire. The handmade sign on the front of the trailer said: *Madame Wanda, Palms and Fortunes*. Madame Wanda herself answered my knock.

"Don't tell me," she called through the closed door. "Let me guess who's there."

"It's me again, from the Health Department. I've got Horgay's dog."

She swung the door open with one arm and held her belly with the other. "I could have predicted that," she said, glad to see me, it seemed. I couldn't take my eyes off the belly straining against the stripes on her shirt. It took a little breath out of me to see her pregnant. "I haven't called the Health Department about this," she added, patting her stomach. "I will though. I see that in my future."

"You're pregnant."

"Can't slip nothing by you Health Department people, can I?" she said and waved me in. The trailer smelled of incense and sausage.

"Ho-el's doing good," she said. "Let me show you... Ho-el!"

He came running. Funny, I didn't remember him even walking the last time I saw him. He looked as though he'd gained some weight. Color was back in his cheeks, a shade that was beginning to match his hair. "Sí, mama, como?" he asked, the syllables rolling off his tongue. I don't think he remembered me, but he stayed put, staring like I was an interesting painting.

"I've got your dog, I think," I said to both him and his mother. I secretly gave Roundabout a little hug, hoping for the artillery report of peanut farts. "You read fortunes?"

"Ain't my dog," she replied. "That dog is some bug Horgay's got up his rear. Sure, I read fortunes. I have the gift."

"Horgay and I spoke this morning."

"See, I already knew that. Horgay!" she yelled.

He came from somewhere in the back, dressed the same as that morning. There they were. The entire family, all in one place, almost posing.

"Hey, Diablo, cómo está?" Horgay called.

Roundabout squirmed under my arm but didn't attempt to jump down. I decided to put him on the floor. He began turning circles but didn't move one way or the other. He couldn't decide which direction to aim his rotations.

"Gracias, ummm . . . señor?" Horgay said, his voice rising more than it should. I knew that tone. It wasn't the first time I'd heard it, the making-fun-of-the-male-nurse tone. Wanda wouldn't put up with that sort of thing. I remembered that punch of hers in the trailer. She owed me one. I had helped her out. I had helped

Ho-El. But the only thing Wanda did was grin, and I knew, right in that second, I was on my own.

"Whatever," I said. I started to go, because that's all I could do, right? I didn't belong there. Horgay said, "So, you are a *nurse*, eh?" Even with my back to them, I could sense him stifling a laugh.

When I turned around, he was in the process of mumbling something to Madame Wanda in Spanish, and she put her hand over her mouth. Horgay repeated the same thing to his son, who started giggling with his father. I didn't have my little Spanish card and wasn't familiar enough with the language to know exactly what he was saying, but I had a pretty good idea. Wanda was having trouble keeping her laughter inside. The stripes across her tight belly danced.

"A very grande nurse, eh?" he said. "A nurse, but one with cajones, eh?"

I must be getting old. I didn't even get pissed. I didn't even consider jacking Horgay's jaw about the nurse cracks. I felt tired all of the sudden, tired and lonely. I knew I should just walk toward the door. Let it all go. Just head out.

As I passed Wanda, I said, "Sometime, I need to let you tell my fortune, Wanda. Tell me what's going to happen."

"Come by anytime," she said, then sucked down a laugh. "Nurse." I shook my head.

She probably didn't know I could have ratted her out to the NASCAR police. Sometimes people don't know the good things you do for them when they aren't looking.

"Sí," Horgay echoed, "and when you are here, you can take all our temperature." They laughed together then, like a chorus. Even Ho-el was in on the joke.

I wondered how good Wanda really was at seeing the future. I wondered if she had a sudden, quick vision, if she foresaw me walking by the open window of the Monte Carlo and spotting keys dangling in the ignition. With arms as long as mine, I had no trouble reaching in and starting the engine. Then another quick twist too far the wrong way, and the key snapped off in the ignition. Did she see that? The Monte Carlo skipped and idled, but stayed running. I thought I heard Roundabout bark inside. I slung the half-key and all of its companions as far as I could in the direction of the railroad tracks. I never heard them hit the ground. The key to the Monte Carlo could still be flying for all I know, for all I care.

But of course, I had no clean getaway. When I turned my own key in the Valiant, the engine spun and the straight pipes fired off like an alarm. The fake fur was beginning to sag from the edges of the windows, and I had to fight to shift the gears into drive. The tires spun a little in the mud, and I weaved my way through the trailers—no dog on the seat beside me, no fortune teller to predict my future, just me, six feet four inches, two hundred and sixty-five pounds, stuck behind the wheel of a car I had no business driving.

The Manila Bond

This is how the end starts. Friday night and I'm sitting at a bar in Manila, Utah. Manila, Utah, is a collection of wind-beaten mobile homes and snow fences jumbled around a crossroads at the chilly, brown edge of the high country. Manila is a dusty place that looks like it will constantly be on the outskirts of something better, but as the Old Man—a staunch advocate for the obvious—said yesterday, "Out here, the distances fool you."

On the western side of the crossroads of Manila sits Sportsman Liquors, a bar that contains more taxidermied deer and antelope heads than customers. Sportsman Liquors is the perfect type of bar to forget the winter or the wind or the circumstances that would bring you to a place like Manila, Utah. Inside, Sportsman Liquors smells of smoke and—swear to God—mothballs. At least I think it's mothballs, that is until I hit the bathroom for the first time and catch the identical smell in my nostrils. I see the mound of crumbling blue cakes in the urinal, and I realize that, more than anything else, Sportsman Liquors smells like a bathroom.

A man sits close on my right, tracing the wood grain with his finger like he's drawing a map in his spilled beer. The stool on my other side is empty, which is funny to me now, since the first punch—actually, the only punch I remember—comes from my left. Luke stands in front of me. Luke, the bartender. Luke, the only null-and-void bartender I've ever encountered. Luke knows nothing. I ask Luke how business has been. "Don't know. Ain't worked in three days." I ask him if this is a good crowd for a Friday. "We don't do crowds," he says.

He is gray-bearded, creases etching his crystal-bright eyes, and I expect old, bright-eyed bartenders to dispense wisdom as well as drafts. So when I ask him what I really want, what I've driven the twenty winding, switch-backed miles into Manila to find, he looks at me across the bar and stares for what feels like a half minute. The mapmaker on my right shifts slightly in his seat. Luke tells me to sit tight, and he walks around the bar, toward a darker section at the rear of Sportsman Liquors. I study the two swallows of beer left in my glass, warm draft that tastes faintly of urinal cakes.

Luke returns to his post behind the bar. "Now, what was that you were looking for again?" he asks, and I repeat my request. Before the question mark lands, something hard and heavy hits me on the bone just below my left ear, and as I fall to the floor of Sportsman Liquors, I notice three things. The guy on my right doesn't move a muscle. One of those deer heads stares at me all the way down. And somebody has duct-taped a blue urinal cake under every single bar stool.

?

Now, you have to go back to Friday morning. The Old Man. God love him. He brought me to Utah to bond and to fly fish. (I have no problem with bonding. I am a strong proponent of bonding. Strong bonding is, probably, good for the soul.) The Old Man was picking up the tab for the trip. What did that make me? A son *and* a prostitute, maybe.

I was not sure we were in need of bonding. We got along fine. But the Old Man, being the Type-A personality, probably saw this as preventative medicine. Bonding, just in case. He'd begun hitting me with the old, "I don't know how many times I'm going to be able to wade these rivers. Better go while we can." And like I said, he footed the bill.

So I was here, with a herd of mostly retired men, my father's fishing buddies who all tied their own flies or talked about tying their own flies. We traveled in a group. I hated group travel, the constant organization and pack-mentality decision-making. These men had names, and so did their flies. The flies were Woolly Buggers and Hot Heads and Chernobyl Ants. The men's names were not as interesting. Joe and Bob and Tom. Nothing as provocative as Bead Head and Royal Wulff.

That Friday morning, I stood thigh-deep in the Green River, whipping the air with a graphite fly rod three feet longer than I was, bonding as best I could. Downstream, I watched my father fight the current with his wading staff. Many men my age had lost their fathers to death or indifference. I counted myself lucky most of the time that he still handled a fly rod and the rapids as well as he did.

I was in the river working hard to make sure the cold, snow-melt current didn't buckle my thighs, worrying more about my bowels than the trout I was spooking. When I travel, I get backed up. Friday morning and I hadn't had a decent crap in four days. Was this important? Yes. It had a bearing on how far I waded into the river. I didn't want to slog too far from the nearest shore in case the dam broke, so to speak.

Upstream from me, Jim Barryman pulled trout after trout from a dark, tiny cut in the current, a small slice of water that ran deeper green. Jim Barryman was nowhere near retirement. Actually, he was only a few years older than I was. He was smarter than the fish he stalked, and they seemed to sense it. They surrendered on the end of his line, curling catatonic in his net. When a brown or rainbow bent his rod, Jim hollered out (rather obviously), "Fish on!" Most everyone within earshot ignored him. I was not that worried about having fish on. I was here for the bonding.

But Jim Barryman felt sorry for me because I hadn't caught any trout. He waved at me just about the time I noticed the drizzle. I'd left my rain jacket in the truck, even after my father reminded me and warned me to stuff it inside my fishing vest. Sometimes, I just don't listen to the things he tells me. As a result, water drooled down my back.

Jim wanted me at his side for a lesson. I knew this because he yelled above the rumble of the current: "Lemme show you something!" I trudged across the slippery rocks to his side. My innards rumbled slightly. A promising sign. The rain fell harder. A mist hovered tight to the warmer air above the river, and a chill worked its way along my wet spine, settling into the bones it could reach.

Jim didn't chit chat. Rather, he inspected the fly tied to the end of my leader. I chose it because of the name: Parachute Adams. It made me think of a cartoon superhero. *Parachute Adams*. Jim said, "You need a Green-Bodied Scud instead of an Adams, and I'll tell you why. Look at the river bottom. See a lot of green grass? That's because they've had low water and lots of sun so far this year. Green grass. What does that tell us?" Before I could fake an answer, he moved on. "Tells me that the fish have probably eaten all of the food supply that is light colored. Now green bugs survived the most, so obviously they would, at this point, be the most plentiful."

Jim threaded the scud onto my leader, and I said this one thing, this one *innocent* comment. I mean, who would suspect? I said, "That's cool. Only the green survive. Natural selection. Darwin would be proud of you." I thought to myself that this observation would be passed among my father's older friends. *Your boy really knows his evolution, huh? That's impressive.* My father would blush with pride. This would add to our bonding experience. But Jim wasn't smiling. He backed away from me like I had a fresh disease and said, "That's wrong. I don't believe in that sort of thing. That's a sin. A sin."

Jim made a hasty, slippery exit toward the near bank, and I was left holding my half-rigged rod. A breeze suddenly picked up and blew a charred odor from the far bank, where an out-of-control wildfire had come to a halt in mid-summer. The burned side of the river resembled the surface of the moon—a desolate, sad gray. The opposite shore grew thick and green; in the evenings, we'd seen deer come to the edge of the river to drink. The rain pelted my back like angry bugs. I was probably still days from a good bowel movement, and it was growing colder by the minute.

?

I don't know how I get from the barroom floor to this narrow room in a narrow building. My guess is that it's a hospital of some kind. Crisp white sheets draped over a cot. A glass-front cabinet stuffed with shelves of cotton balls and jars of tongue depressors within reaching distance. A desk sits at the front of the long, skinny room and above the desk—honest to God—a stuffed mule deer head. Not the same one that eyed me on my way toward the floor of Sportsman Liquors, but the two could be kin, they look so much alike.

I feel like I have a hangover, but I didn't drink enough for a headache of *this* magnitude. Yes, I was moderately buzzed when I left my dad and his buddies at the lodge and headed for the bar in Manila. But this pain begins in the distinct neighborhood of my left ear. Then I remember the smack on the head. Through a dusty window, I see the weather's broken and the sun is out. Which means I've been here through the night. Which means the Old Man's crazy worried, especially since I have his rental car. I wonder how this all impacts the rules of group travel? Do they send out a search party or just go fishing? The Old Man is too old to tackle fears like this, and guilt suddenly flows through me like ice water.

I assume I'm not alone, that somewhere else sits a doctor, ready to care for me. The moment I begin to roll over on my side is when I feel the knives under my chest and notice the tight wrapping wound around my ribs. And when I groan, *that's* when I realize my jaw is wired shut. I've never had my jaw wired before. All I can do is grunt and moan like an animal, a sad mule deer, maybe. I lever myself to a sitting position, ribs scalding inside the wrapping, and my brain sloshes inside my skull. I try to suck in more air, and it feels as though someone is perched on my chest, even though I'm upright on the cot. I can't remember how I got this way. I see now that I'm in a double-wide trailer.

In the small pauses between the banging sounds in my ears, I hear footsteps crunch outside. A woman walks in holding a plastic ketchup bottle. A solid woman. She could take on a high-country wind, but she's not overweight. Just substantial. And she's dressed as if she's going out on the town. I can't imagine where that would be in Manila, Utah, early on a Saturday morning.

"Well, well," she says. "You're awake, you're awake. Good, good." I wonder if she echoes herself every time she speaks.

I want to tell her I can't talk. The sounds come out like a foreign language. Fortunately, she is aware of the situation.

"I went down to The Skillet and grabbed one of their squirt bottles. I thought you could use it to eat something. Cream of Wheat or some such. I'm Darcy, the nurse." She holds the bottle toward me like a handshake. "I have to get to church. I'll check back after the ten thirty service." She lays the squirt bottle down on the cotton ball cabinet.

My head spins, and I ease back on the cot. Church means Sunday. I drove to Manila on a Friday night. I'm trying to connect the chronological dots when Darcy comes back through the door. "Almost forgot," she says. "Your dad will be right back. He just went for some breakfast at The Skillet."

The Old Man, eating an egg-white omelet and home fries all by himself, I think and wait for the banging to quiet in my head.

?

Back to that Friday afternoon. The rain finally brought fishing to a halt. The Old Man tossed me a towel. My teeth chattered, and I shivered like a nervous dog. "I told you to bring a rain jacket. They give you one towel a day and can't give you a lousy mixing bowl." He was still pissed that our tiny cabin was ill-equipped. "You should've just gone back to the truck when it started."

"I couldn't leave. Jim was showing me something," I said.

"Nice fellow. He's always happy to share his knowledge."

"He shared a little something else, too." I stopped toweling off my head and let that bit of info float out into the air.

The Old Man stared into one of his many-chambered fly boxes, checking the ammo for tomorrow. "Hmmm?" he murmured, faking interest.

I forged ahead, despite the fact he couldn't care less that I tweaked Jim Barryman's old-time religion. "I said something about Darwin and natural selection, and he acted like I'd broken a commandment."

This got his attention. "How so?"

"He said he doesn't talk about that sort of thing. Says it's a sin."

"Well, he's real biblical," the Old Man said.

"He went all cable-channel Christian on me for a second," I said.

"Best to just let it lie. You don't know these guys all that well. Take a shower. You'll warm up, then we'll go grab something to eat. The guys are meeting at the lodge for dinner. Nobody feels like grilling tonight, what with the rain and all." He closed his fly box. He was a good man, really. More enlightened than most of his fishing buddies. I could have done much worse for a father.

?

Darcy's squirt bottle reminds me how hungry I am. Her mention of Cream of Wheat makes my stomach growl, a strange occurrence considering my travel-induced constipation. I notice I'm not wearing my pants. Instead of the jeans I wore Friday night, I have on a pair of thick wool work pants that are way too large through the waist. I blush with the thought that my fall to the floor may have shaken the whole system loose, but I can't be too embarrassed about something I never actually witnessed.

The squirt bottle is cold to the touch, filled with a chocolate milkshake, I imagine. My stomach creaks. I find a place to insert the nozzle of the squirt bottle between my molars, and I squeeze quick and hard. I wait for the shake—chocolate, I hope—to fill my mouth, but all I get is disappointment. The bottle contains something with the consistency of tartar sauce, but actually a little thinned-down and too runny to be real tartar sauce. The taste of tin and decay washes over my tongue. I want to clear my throat and spit so badly my eyes begin to tear. The heaves start, and I hear myself hack a sound not unlike a cat working up a hairball. You never realize how hard it is to spit something out of your mouth when your jaw is wired shut. I don't have any choice but to swallow a mouthful of what must have been a condiment in a former, fresher life. Darcy must have picked up the wrong squirt bottle.

The heaves begin to slow, and I hear more footsteps on the trailer porch. The Old Man walks in, carrying a Styrofoam cup and a long straw. "Coke," he says, "with crushed ice. Thought you might like a little something sweet if you woke up."

He doesn't ask questions, doesn't try to make conversation, just watches me suck down the entire cup of soda, washing away any reminders of the squirt bottle. He waits patiently until I'm through, then after a deep, long breath, says, "Why didn't you tell me?"

I make the sound of a question mark.

"I mean, I can't say it's not a total surprise. Probably will kill your mother. But you and me, I mean, I thought you would have told *me* before now."

I ask him what the hell he's talking about, but the words emerge in little blasts of sound and sharp snorts of air through my teeth. I look around for something to write with.

He says, "I don't understand why you felt like you had to do something on a Friday night. Why couldn't you wait until you got home? I mean, I don't know much about this sort of lifestyle. I suppose this explains you still being a bachelor and all. Every once in a while, your mother will read me something about it from Dear Abby. I'm guessing the urges come on you all of the sudden, and you have to be off on your own, doing what you do? But Jesus, a little self-control, especially in front of my friends, that's all I'm saying. A little control."

I study his face. It's like he's speaking German. I'm so lost.

"And why Black? Not that I'm a racist or anything, but why Black? The sheriff said that the whole Black thing sort of added fuel to the fire. That's what made those guys really kick your ass. You know what? Doesn't matter. You're my boy, my son. I'll love you no matter what. Damn, I sound like one of those movies your mother watches on television. Well, I mean it, so there." He reaches over and pats me on the head like he used to do when I was seven and brought home a report card full of As.

Just behind the squirt bottle is a prescription pad and a pen advertising some sort of drug. In the blank space where the doctor fills in the information, I write: *What in God's name are you talking about?*

He reads it, and disappointment floods his face. "It's out now," he says. "You don't have to pretend. I mean, you don't walk into a bar in Manila, Utah and start asking people where you can find a Black homosexual and expect things to stay under wraps, son. It's okay. Really okay."

?

Friday evening, and the special at the Red Canyon Lodge was a Seafood Risotto with salmon, scallops, and clams. Seafood a thousand miles from the nearest ocean. I opted for the chicken fried steak. Strange, I never saw trout on the menu. There were eight of us at the table. Everyone cleaned up after the muddy, rainy day on the river. The various colognes mingled and fought in the air over the table. Old Spice versus Brut versus Mennen.

The fish stories began to fly after the waitress delivered the drinks. I was the only one hammering beers. There were a couple of vodka tonics, but mostly waters and iced teas and coffee. Lying is a fishing tradition, and the least skillful fishermen are the most adroit liars. I would have called *that* natural selection if the topic weren't taboo.

Anyway, I was deep into my fourth Bud when the guy across from my father (Lester, I think his name was) said something about going to Disney World. I missed how the conversation spun in that direction. Lester said *Disney World*, and Jim Barryman perked up.

"Well, be careful, that's all I've got to say. Sara just bought us tickets to take the kids. She called down there to ask them what big groups had reservations. You know what I mean…" Jim Barryman paused to sip at his water and peered over the top of his glass.

I was about to say something to join the conversation, something valuable and engaging. Like, *Hey, to avoid the big groups, you really ought to go in the fall.* I'd been so quiet to this point. I wanted to contribute. But Jim didn't give me the opportunity.

"No way I'm spending money going down there at the same time one of those groups is showing up. Especially with kids around," he said. "We have to protect our kids, am I right?"

The table nodded at him like they knew the code. (All nodded, I'm proud to say, *except* me and the Old Man. He fished with these guys, but he didn't fall into lockstep with them all the time. That gave me hope.) "So Sara asked the person on the phone, 'Hey, can you tell me what big groups are going to be there?' and can you believe she wouldn't tell her?"

"You're kidding," someone said at the other end of the table, like an audience plant.

"They have some privacy policy about telling who's coming," Jim said.

Lester had it figured. "Still leftover 9/11 stuff. They don't want some terrorist coming down and bombing Mickey Mouse." Nods all around.

Jim continued. "So Sara, God bless her, says, 'Hey, listen you, I've got a five-year-old and an infant, and I'll be darned if I'm taking them to Disney World when you've got some giant gay or lesbian mob running all over the Magic Kingdom.'"

At that point, I was beginning to see things through a Budweiser filter, but—I hasten to add—my hearing was in perfect working order. The floodgates opened, and Jim had spun the valves. Around the table, men began venting their outrage at the existence of homosexuals through a variety of methods, mostly the usual, like,

"My wife works with a couple of gays, and they're fine in the office. Good workers, good workers." Or, "You know, we had one in our neighborhood and he pretty much kept to himself, and as long as they keep to themselves, well, that's fine by me."

Then, Jim said, "For a while, we had a gay in our neighborhood, and he had a Negro boyfriend and the two of them took walks every evening. I couldn't have the kids outside in the front yard when they took their little strolls. Makes me so damn mad. And you know what? They try to say that they can't help it, that it's a genetic thing. But it isn't and you know why? Because if it was a gene, it would have died out. Gays can't reproduce, and when you don't reproduce, genes die out. That's the way it works."

I looked over at my father. I was already rising in my seat, ready to remind Jim Barryman that what he had just stated was down-and-dirty evolutionary theory that would make Darwin smile. And, of course, I'd have to call him a fucking hypocrite as a postscript. The Old Man stared across the top of his iced tea and raised one eyebrow and shook his head slightly. He knew what I was thinking. Without talking, he was saying, *Don't take that bait. We've still got a few days of fishing left. Let it go.*

So, I bit my tongue. For real. I know people say that, but I actually bit mine. It didn't hurt. I ordered another beer and, when the waitress delivered it, I whispered that she should probably go ahead and bring a couple more while she was at it, to save some steps.

The conversation gained momentum, each man giving testimony about brushes with the gay community or the Black community or the gay/Black community, until the entrées arrived. By that time, I'd had more than a six pack. The Old Man watched me but knew better than to draw attention to my collection of empty bottles that the waitress seemed to ignore.

I picked at the chicken fried steak and listened to the snatches of dialogue that filtered into my ears. Talk of sin and sodomy and Bible verses and immigrants that "ought to learn English, by God." Another swallow of beer, and I headed for the bathroom to pee. The Old Man turned in his chair and watched me leave.

I weaved in front of the urinal, staring at Polaroid pictures tacked on the wall—men cradling huge trout, men who had stayed at the Red Canyon Lodge, smiling white men—and when I hitched my pants to zip them, I noticed I had the key to our rental car in my front pocket. This was where it went bad. I should have thought it through, done some analysis. But I was inspired by the keys in my pocket. The plan rushed in on me all at once, and I thought it was so brilliant I wanted to squeal.

That precise moment, I decided to leave the men at the table in the Red Canyon Lodge and drive the tight, meandering road to Manila. I pledged to myself I would sniff around in the traditional places and somehow, somewhere find a Black man who was gay, and I would bring him back to the Red Canyon Lodge. Tomorrow morning, I would stick him in a pair of waders and stand him on the riverbank, right in front of Jim Barryman, and I would say, "Here's one, Jim. Now, how about you acting like Jesus and teaching him to fish, you motherfucker."

It was one of those alcohol-fueled ideas that seemed good at only one precise moment in time, in one particular place. I snuck through the back door of the kitchen before I lost my train of thought, grabbing two beers from the cooler beside the bar on my way out. Nobody working in the kitchen noticed. I don't think anybody really cared.

❓

After Darcy finishes with church, she sends me on my way. Gives me a little paper sack full of Tylenol 4's and photocopied instructions about how to take care of my teeth while my jaw is wired. She tells me to be sure and see my doctor, and maybe even my dentist, as soon as I get home. She hands me a big yellow envelope filled with X-rays of my jaw, which I am scared to open. I have no desire to see photos of broken-down, wired-up things.

I want to ask her where my pants are and whose pants I'm wearing and who I need to pay for the pants, but it's too much of an effort to sift the words through my teeth. And I don't feel like writing. I suppose if they need repayment, they'd ask for it. I'm guessing my pants are long gone in a local dumpster.

Outside, the October sun beats down on Manila, light bouncing off the aluminum trailers, too much light for my eyes to soak in. The brightness pinballs inside my head as well, putting a shiny, sharp edge on my constant headache. The rental car idles in front of the hospital trailer. I see Darcy watching us from the window. She waves as we pull away, her big, solid hand filling an entire pane of glass.

On the slow forty-minute drive back to the Red Canyon Lodge, I want to tell the Old Man the whole story, but the words stay behind my teeth. Instead, I write it down for him on a prescription pad I slipped into the pocket of somebody else's pants.

On paper, I tell the Old Man I'd had too much beer and too much Bible School at the dinner table. I pencil in that I left to find Jim Barryman a new fly-fishing partner, a Black man with an elegant cast who could really fill out a pair of waders. I write down that *I'm sorry you had to hunt for me*. Write down that I'm too old to make him worry like that. Write down that *I got Darcy's phone number* because *she is one hot Manilan*.

Ha, ha, I write, finally.

I hold the pad up for him to see. He glances quickly, laughs, then says that sons are never too old to make their fathers worry. "Comes with the territory," he says. He adds that I can do much better than Darcy, if that's the kind of thing I'm really, truly looking for.

We pull up to the little row of cedar-log cabins just beyond the woods next to the Red Canyon Lodge, the gravel crunching beneath the tires. The Old Man's friends cluster around a table on the porch of one of the cabins, tying new flies they hope will work that afternoon. I wonder what he's told them about my weekend adventure. I'm suddenly so sorry I've embarrassed him, I want to cry.

The Old Man cuts the engine. "Jim said he was going to pray for you to find your way. He's going to ask God to help you," he says, smiling. "So hey, you got that going for you."

I suspect God is too busy patrolling the long lines at Disney World or perusing the beige suburbs where dangerous gay couples stroll around the block before sundown, or He's over at Sportsman Liquors where the barstools smell like the inside of a janitor's closet. God does not have time for single men who can't fish or can't hold their domestic beer or who make bad decisions weaving over a urinal.

The Old Man reaches for the door, and I grab his sleeve.

Through the tiny open spaces in my teeth, I tell him that we should sit here for a minute, just sit still in the car and let those guys on the porch see what it looks like when a couple of men really bond.

Let them all wonder.

Taps on the Forehead

Used to be, wasn't a thing between me and this blackwater river but a few big knothole widow-maker trees and swamp and cypress knees and wasn't a thing living here but a couple raccoon families in the knotholes and a wild hog I could hear most mornings rooting with his nose down in the mud and his ass cranked up in the air. Two hot summers in a row, though, and the swamp changed like swamps will do when left on their own. Dried-up mud and junkweed and stinking like a hot dump. But it was a quiet place, and I could hear that hog hunting for a mud hole deep enough to cool off his nuts. Then, one day it isn't quiet anymore. Some man buys up a chunk of the riverfront and stakes out the foundation of a house with a little piss ant hammer so brand new, it shines when it hits the sun.

He drives a green car with a sticker on the bumper that tells him where to park. I hate shit such as that—stickers that tell you what you can do or what you can't. I got nothing against a sticker of the US of A flag or a Bible verse or something like that, but people with parking stickers, they think they are better than other people. They think they worth more because they got a space all to their own.

I stand behind a thick pine at the back corner of my place and watch. The man studies a piece of paper spread across the hood of that car. He pulls a measuring tape out his pocket and walks off some distance, then pounds a stake in the ground. He stretches a string tight between another stake and before the afternoon is half over, he's laid out a house among the trees. Doesn't look like much of a house. Looks more like some giant cat's cradle gone bad. But it's enough to piss me off, him standing there seeing stuff in his head that's going to mess up my life.

He's got a German shepherd that follows him around like a toy on a pull string. The dog catches wind of me, sticks his nose in the air, and bristles his back in my direction, but Sticker Man doesn't even turn. "Hush, fella, now," is all he says. There isn't twenty feet between me and him and that dog.

So, he's going to build him a house.

I got no need for a house. I got my trailer. I bought it from a fellow after it'd been burned. Just on one side. Big fucking deal. Looking at it made me think of a potato somebody forgot to turn in the oven. Cost me four hundred dollars, and I had to tow it here myself. But I did it all on my own, and it's up on cement blocks now so it sits level. I have lived in it going on four-and-a-half years now, and I have been happy as I can expect. In summer, I open the windows at both ends of the trailer, and a breeze blows through the screens all night long. Sounds like a sewing machine running. In winter, I shut everything up tight and stuff towels under the door jambs and along the window frames, turn the kerosene heater on low, and it gets so warm, I break a sweat before daylight.

I got a trailer, I got a mailbox out by the road, and I got enough space around me, I can walk out on the little two-step porch buck naked if I want to and take me a piss on the cement blocks. It's different now. There's a man with a dog between me and the river.

"Hey," I say and step out from around my tree. Damn German shepherd shows me his teeth, so I'll know he has them. Dogs don't ever waste time letting you know how they feel. Most honest motherfuckers in the world.

"Well, hello," Sticker Man says, dropping the string and stakes and hammer and sticking out his hand, like shaking hands is going to make us best buddies. Fuck him. "Smith McCuen," he says, his hand floating there, a bird in the wind. His fingers are blue from the chalk line he's been stringing. "Just bought this plot. Doing some preliminary things today. Beautiful land here. I think I'll take down some of these trees today. Open things up a bit." He lets a long breath out. A couple of mosquitoes dogfight around his ears.

He's so damn happy you'd think he just got laid. I don't trust people who have to use a last name for their first one. I leave his hand hanging until he pulls it back. That smile on his face twitches. "And you are...?" he asks me and reaches down and pats his dog on the head.

"I'm the man come to tell you to keep that dog off my land." I show my teeth a little, especially to the dog. So he'll know I own a set, too.

"Pardon?"

"I got a shotgun," I say. The man smiles. Him and his dog must brush their teeth at the same time. He talks low and calm and bats at one of the mosquitoes.

"Oh, now, Fritz is a gentle fellow. He wouldn't hurt anyone. Even you. He never bothers a soul. No need for talk about guns and animals."

"You just keep that in mind," I say, and his smile disappears like somebody walked up and erased it from a chalkboard.

"Now, look here—" His patience runs dry. I know I'm winning when that happens.

I say, "I ain't got to *look* at nothing I don't want to, and I don't want to look at no dog or no new house or nobody stomping around so close to my trailer. And I'm going to take a nap, so don't start up that chainsaw." I can see the man turn into somebody different right in front of me, which is good. Folks don't like to change on the spur of the moment.

"You're the guy in the trailer," he says, peering over my shoulder to see it. It's just inside the tree line. Can't see it until you walk up on it. It blends in like it belongs there. "I've heard about you."

I'd love to know what people say about me when I can't hear them. The only person I know stupid enough to talk about me behind my back is Trudy, my wife until she decided she'd had enough of the two of us. She has spent the last two years waiting on tables, trying to forget who I am. But her biggest problem is, she can't forget who *she* is, an ex-wife who's getting older and staying single and working for tips.

Every chance she gets, Trudy shovels people an earful of what a worthless dickhead I am. When those stories eventually float down the river to where I live, I try to shut her up, but every time I go near her, she screams and holds up her waitress ink pen like a little knife, then the cook calls the sheriff and the sheriff eventually shows up at my door.

But this Sticker Man won't quit talking. I wonder if he's nervous. "I heard you lived in this area and that you would be by, to check out who I was and what I was up to. Well, I already told you who I am. And what am I up to? I'm up to building a house. My house on my land, accompanied by my dog, who, by the way, is very well-trained, if you know what I mean." He tries to give me a look like he's tough, tries to make his eyes go hard like ol' Clint Eastwood and make his breath come in puffs, but you can look at his hands and tell he isn't tough at all. Under the blue dust, they are soft and white as little pillows. I'll bet he sleeps on his hands. Bet he uses lotion on them.

"You're not building any house here," I tell him.

"Just watch me," he says.

"I aim to, mister," I say, which I think sounds like it came from a movie, it sounds so good. Clint Eastwood. I can do Clint better than Clint can. It sounds like I'm not scared of anything short of a bolt of God's lightning. He stares at his hands when he hears me, but I walk off before he has a chance to answer. Ten minutes later, he's packed up and gone back where he came from, and I flip a bird at his dust.

?

Next morning, Raymond's at my door, banging it so his high school ring hits on the wood strip. I see his Crown Vic idling through the window.

"I haven't gone near Trudy!" I yell at the door.

"Yeah, but you went and bothered that guy building the house."

"So?"

"Not too neighborly of you."

"I don't want neighbors," I say. We're doing all of this through the door.

"You got no choice. He bought the land. He can do what he wants on it, within reason, you know. Now, if you keep on with him, I'm gonna have to take you into town."

I can't say a thing. That may be true about his land, but I don't have to like it. "For what?" I say. "Not a law in the land against speaking your peace. That's covered in the Pledge of Allegiance or something."

Raymond stops for a second because he knows I got a point, then I hear him from the other side of the door. "You leave him alone, hear? Let him build his house. And don't you so much as think about taking target practice on his dog. Anyway, you aren't supposed to have a gun, what with your parole."

Parole. Shit. About the most confusing thing the world can do to a man is stick his ass on parole. I can't remember what I'm supposed to do or not do on parole. Sit the wrong way on the commode, they haul you in for breaking parole. So many rules. Makes me feel like I'm back in high school.

What happened was, Trudy had a date one night with some pretty boy right after we split up, and I ended up beating on the guy's head. I didn't want to tune him up that bad, but he kept laughing when I hit him. I wanted to make him stop laughing. He didn't die, which was good. Trudy couldn't go out with him again because he left town straight from the hospital. He didn't look the same. Eighteen months, aggravated assault. And then that damn parole. When I finally got back to my trailer, a whole group of possums had taken up in the kitchen.

"I don't have so much as a water pistol. I was just talking. Can't hurt anybody with just words."

"Well, you can sure scare the shit out of them. Just leave him be."

"Fine," I say and nod my head, which he can't see, of course.

"Fine and dandy," he yells back and stomps off the porch. "I better not hear about any goddamn gun."

?

My daddy always called me the worst kind of pest. *You make people crazy*, was what he said. What I think he meant was, I make people do things they feel bad about the next day. I've made school teachers run right out the door, hit their knees, and cry in the hall until the bell rings. I've made cousins claim we aren't kin. I've made women wish they never laid eyes on me.

It's a secret, knowing how to make people crazy. The secret is, it's not about big things. You don't have to hit people over the head with a hammer to make them crazy. You just got to tap them on the forehead with a pencil about six hundred times in a row. What I'm saying is, you don't have to be strong or quick. You just got to be mean and keep at it.

I go over after dark the next day, and I stand there looking at the string he spent all afternoon stretching. It shines like spider webs in the light my old Coleman lantern throws. I can't decide whether to move the stakes a little or just cut the string. I do both. I pile the stakes in the middle of his invisible house and ball up the leftover string. Then I start me a bonfire that isn't all that big, but it gets hot enough and makes the trees look like they are alive. I cut off the lantern to save on fuel.

Next morning, Sticker Man pulls up and looks at the pile of black coals in the middle of his land. He sticks his neck out toward my direction, unclips his dog from a leash, and starts staking up his house again. He doesn't even think twice about it, just starts right up with the measuring and the pounding with his shiny hammer. No cussing or anything. It takes him until the middle of the afternoon to get the first bunch of lines pulled. It turns hotter, and the gnats come out. He sweats all the way through one t-shirt and peels it off, and now he's turning pink, slapping at bugs on his bare back. He won't last here long, neither will that dog of his if it keeps walking the edge of my property, that long limp-dick tongue of his hanging pink out of his mouth.

Seeing the two of them working so hard makes me thirsty, so I decide to take the truck to town. I am not worried. Sticker Man wouldn't dare fuck with me or my stuff. He's too nice for that. I got a craving for a beer and a Chocolate Soldier. I started drinking the two of them together when I was still in high school. Out in the parking lot during lunch, I'd have me a bottle of Chocolate Soldier in my hand and a cold beer tucked behind my back. Sip the Soldier when the teacher came walking by. Sip the beer when the coast was clear. The combo grew on me.

Stimey keeps me a case of Chocolate Soldiers behind the bar. Usually sees me coming and has me set up by the time I hit the door. Inside The Cotton Bottom, there are no light bulbs in the light sockets and the air's always thick with the stink from the night before. The only glow comes from the jukebox and the neon Miller High Life sign buzzing behind the bar.

Stimey starts talking to me before my eyes get used to the dark. "Trudy says you about to step on your pecker again, says you gonna end up slow dancing with some fudge packer down at county."

Haven't taken my first sip yet, and he's already fucking with me. I hate bartenders.

"Messing with that professor the way you did," he says. "Lord, lord..."

"Professor?"

"What bought the land next to yours," Stimey says.

"Professor?" I say again.

"At the college. The girl's school."

"I've seen those girls before, walking around town." They are always in little groups, coveys of quail.

"He teaches history, somebody said," Stimey says.

"How do you know all this?" I say.

"Son, if I don't hear it firsthand, then I hear it from somebody who heard it firsthand. Trudy told me all about the professor. She waits on him at the diner. Trudy says you're an idiot. Says you going to wind up back in jail, where you belong."

The Chocolate Soldier is empty, and there's only a sip of beer left. Stimey ducks down to grab another round. "I quit caring what Trudy says a good while back," I tell him.

"Yeah, like hell you did," he says.

"Fuck you," I say.

"Hey, I'm the only one who can use language like that in my place, so shut up. You want a glass?" He knows I don't ever use a glass. He's just trying to get another rise out of me.

It turns dark outside while I drink and drink and don't pee and get a buzz so good I think I can catch bullets or dodge cars—one of those immortality, you-can't-kill-me buzzes. I walk by the diner and there's Trudy through the window, smiling while she pours coffee, bending over and stretching her blue uniform on the backside. She doesn't see me, which is good. When I am drunk, I don't win any of the arguments I start.

Behind the diner, in the gravel parking lot, I find her rusty Plymouth Duster. I want to leave her something, so she'll know I have been there and know I could've made a scene. If I had paper, I could leave a note. Her car is backed into a parking space, with enough room between the bumper and the wall for me to pee. When I'm not weaving and blocking the light from the telephone pole, I see she's got a goddamn parking sticker, just like The Professor. I keep swaying in and out of the light, so the sticker looks like it's blinking at me. Winking at me. I hate stickers. I hate it that Trudy has one. Through that window, she doesn't look as big as she used to be. I hate that too. If she goes and messes around and gets skinny and happy, I'm liable to kill somebody. I end up pissing all over my shoes.

The sticker won't peel off, so I break off both of her windshield wipers, snap them free like dead twigs. I shove them up her tailpipe. The next time it rains, I hope she goes blind trying to find the fucking road.

?

He must have heard my truck leave. Fucker. Heard me leave and figured I wouldn't be back for a long time. That was a gamble. I could have been just going to the store.

While I was gone, he took down a half dozen trees around his house site, it looks like, then, at some point, walked his dog right up on my little two-step porch and let him drop a load. He did say that his dog was trained, *if you know what I mean.*

That dog's been eating well. Leaves a pile of shit so big, you'd swear a cow'd been visiting my trailer. Leaves it right where I'll step in it too. I see it before I smell it, but what with all the beer and Chocolate Soldiers, my piss-covered feet are under their own control. Right smack in it I go, like stepping into mud. When I was a kid, we had a big old hunting dog that used the whole backyard as his private shithole. We'd step in stuff all day long. Never bothered me then, and if he thinks it bothers me now, he's dumber than I thought. He may know history, but he doesn't know mine. I just leave my shoes in the yard and go to sleep. In the morning, everything will be dry and easy to scrape off with a kitchen knife.

?

I sleep through the next morning until I think my head is done pounding. I hear him out there, banging stakes and whistling to his dog every once in a while.

My stomach feels like I sucked down a quart of drain opener. Sometimes the beer and the chocolate don't mix right. The inside of my mouth feels like it's grown hair. I'd pay ten dollars for a big soda with crushed ice right now. If I was with Trudy, she'd bring it to me in bed. She would do little things like that every now and again.

The banging stops and an engine cranks up. I think it might be one of them weed whacker things until the sound moves up the road. It's his car. He's gone, and when I peek out the window of my trailer, I see he left by himself. His dog is still here, walking back and forth along my property line like a freaking Marine. He doesn't take his eyes off my trailer, and when I go out on the back steps in my underwear, the dog stops walking the whole time I'm peeing. Those ears are up and cocked back just a little. He sniffs the air and never stops staring.

I take an old lawn chair from under the trailer and put it out in front, and me and that dog watch each other for an hour. I sweat beer and chocolate and smell like the inside of a boot, but the only reason I leave my chair is to get a new beer. I didn't have any soda in the refrigerator. And what with the sun and the beer, pretty soon I have an encore buzz coming on. I just wish I had a Chocolate Soldier or two. I try tricking the dog with niceness, calling out to him and smacking my lips, trying to get him to walk in the yard, but he's having none of it.

I shut my eyes when the sun gets up high, and I have a foggy dream about that dog. I dream he comes tiptoeing across the line and sniffs at the bottoms of my feet, then starts licking my toes, which doesn't feel too bad, only tickles some when his tongue flicks around my foot and my ankle. Makes me twitch. The dog is smiling at me, like he's going to tickle me to death.

I start laughing in my sleep so hard from the dream-tickling that I wake up, and when I look down, I see what the tickling was all about. I got a whole goddamn army of fire ants making their way around my feet and up my leg. The minute I jump out the chair, they get mad and start biting and before I can get to the hose pipe and wash them off, they bite into the hide on my leg all the way from the ankle to the knee. It hurts so bad the only thing I can do is throw up, and that dog never takes his eyes off me the whole time.

When the sun starts going down behind the trees, I've still got the sweats from all the ant bites, but they feel better since I rubbed corn syrup all over them. It's that dog's damn fault I got stung a million times. I got lessons to show him.

My bass rod is under the porch. It's rigged with forty-pound test that is so strong I could pull over small trees with it. In the bottom of my tackle box, in amongst the split shot and broken pieces of rubber worms, I find the biggest treble hook I got. I tie it on my line and bury it deep inside a piece of leftover hamburger steak I find in the refrigerator. The dog doesn't have any idea. Probably thinks I'm going catfishing or something.

I move my chair closer to the tree line and make sure I don't set up over an ant hill. I get close enough to drive that dog crazy. Don't want to make him mad because with my leg the way it is, I couldn't outrun a newborn baby. I check the drag on my reel, then cast the piece of meat in his direction. He backs up a few steps in the dirt. I flip it again and again, a couple of feet closer each cast. Oh, he wants to know what it tastes like. He wants to know bad. He looks at me, then at the meat, then at me. He can't make up his mind.

Finally, I'm tossing it right in front of him. It's almost dark now. He's seeing with his nose. I know he hasn't eaten all day, unless he snuck off while I was sleeping. The light is getting bad. I can hear the meat hit the ground, but I lose sight of it in the air. I'm getting close, I know. I am a patient man. I been fishing all my life, and I haven't found a bass yet that can outwait me.

He sniffs one of my casts. I can barely see his nose right on it. I'm talking to him, the same way I talk to the fish when I'm in the river. "Go ahead, sonuvabitch, you hungry, you know you hungry. Big bite." He sniffs and walks away. I reel in the meat, check the hook, and toss again. He can't stand it.

This time he picks up the meat and carries it real soft, like he's stole a raw egg, and he starts walking toward the center of the property. I give him plenty of line. The meat's still in his teeth. Just like a damn largemouth bass, he has to go get some privacy before he can swallow good. Won't bring himself to chew in public.

I can barely make out his shape. He stops and puts the meat on the ground. Watches it for a second. I twitch the line. Then he gobbles it, throws his head back and sucks it down his throat.

He knows right away he's fucked. He starts running for the woods, not making any noise, and the line zips off my reel, sounding like a mad beehive. I'm still patient. "I am going break your fucking back," I tell him. "I am going jerk your stomach through your fucking teeth." I let him take line until I'm down to the last fifty feet or so, and I plant my heels in the dirt, throw the drag, and snatch that dog blind from the goddamn pain.

He howls like a ghost. The drag doesn't even slow him down, so I tighten it. I am not worried about the line breaking. That's why I use forty-pound test. The line goes slack. He's backtracking on me. I reel as fast as my wrist will spin. I take out the slack and set the hook again, and I can see him now, running circles in the property, rolling on his back, cutting flips in the air. I feel like I'm on a goddamn fishing show. He's howling, wishing he was dead. I got the butt of the rod between my legs, and the thing is bent over like fucking pulp wood in a hurricane. The dog takes off for the woods again. I know he isn't hooked in the lip because he isn't shaking his head trying to throw it out. I take out my pocket knife and cut him loose.

That'll be the last time somebody puts a dog on their property to keep an eye on me. Goddammit.

?

Raymond is back the next day and starts in with more of his questions.

I say, "I ain't been outside this trailer since yesterday morning. Since them ants tried to carry me off." I pull my pants leg up, and Raymond squints his eyes. He's been bit before, so he knows what it looks like.

"You ought to watch where you're stepping. Looks like you been hit with number nine shot," he says.

"I fell asleep in my chair," I say.

"He hasn't seen his dog since yesterday morning. I told him I own a coon dog that stays out weeks at a time chasing nookie, but he said his dog wouldn't do that kind of thing. He says he told the dog to stay in the yard, and the dog does everything he tells it to."

Raymond doesn't have his heart in it. I can see it in his eyes. The man next door is starting to get on his nerves, too. The Professor is turning into a pain in the ass. Raymond wishes he'd go away, just like me.

"Well, I'm sure glad you're taking care of this, Raymond. I'm glad there isn't anything more important to do than this. Fuck all them gangs and rapers and car thieves. Did I miss it or they make you dog catcher, too?" I say.

"You shoot that dog?" he asks me, but he doesn't care.

"Shot him and ate him for supper. Tough fucker. Hard to chew and chew. I got some leftovers inside. You had lunch?" I smile.

"You're so damn funny. What isn't going to be funny is if you did something to that guy's dog. He's pretty pissed right now."

My heart starts beating a little faster, but I'm not about to let anybody know it. "And what's he gonna do? Come over here and whip my ass? Hell, only thing he can whip is his own dick," I say.

Raymond digs around in his ear with the key to his police car. He looks tired. "Why you got to be like this?"

"Like what?"

"Like such trash. All you got left in your life is a bad attitude. You weren't like this before Trudy left. You need to get you somebody, if that's what'll keep you from being such trash. Find you a woman. Or buy a TV set or something. Move on in life," he says.

Raymond always works her into a conversation, one way or the other. "You think Trudy's my problem? Says who? Trudy? She's nothing to me. You see, Raymond, you start believing everything that woman says, you'll end up like me. Goddamn, she's just like a weather girl on TV. She says something and everybody believes it."

"I hope you didn't hurt that dog," Raymond says, staring me right in the eyes, trying to pick up on a tell.

"Hope is a silly thing, officer," I say, but he knows I'm fucking with him.

"I'll be back. I'll be sure and tell Trudy you're about the same as always. She asks about you, you know? And sometimes she really wants to know how you doing."

That sort of thing could bother me, knowing somebody actually wonders about me, but I just tell Raymond, "Too little, too late." Sounds like something ol' Clint would say about an ex-wife.

?

They never find the dog, but Sticker Man knows I did it. He knows because all I do is wave at him now, while he digs the footings for his house. I am too friendly. I call him "neighbor" out loud and on purpose, and he hasn't said a word to me in three weeks. He had some men out to clear the rest of the trees. He works on the house in the late afternoon, until dark, then he climbs in his car and drives off.

I don't even go over there when he's gone. I mean, I could fill in his newest holes and cut his string or stomp in his wet cement, but I'm driving him crazy without breaking a sweat. I'm tapping him on the forehead with that pencil. Me, the pest. I feel like a new person because I'm winning this fight even though a house is going up, and when I'm winning, I don't need anything else in the world from nobody.

One Sunday night, he comes driving back to his land around ten o'clock. That's different for him, being around that late at night. From inside my trailer, I watch the headlights bouncing through the trees, and when he turns the car off, there's music playing loud, making thumping noises. *Boombaddaboombaddaboom.* It's country music. He opens the door and the music gets louder, and I see two heads, one of them is a woman, and they're both giggling and singing along with the songs they know. So Sticker Man has a girl.

He lights a camping lantern and hangs it on a two-by-four stuck in the ground. They start dancing in the circle of light. When they stop, she ducks inside the car and pulls out a little cooler. The way it sounds, the last thing those two need is another one. I want to tell him to be careful. Too much of that stuff in the cooler, and he won't be able to get it up. I'm almost proud of him, having a woman over there. Makes him more like somebody I could get to know.

The woman pops the top on something and hollers at him. "Bottoms up, Big Boy," and my breath catches in my throat like a fish bone. "There you go!" She's still hollering.

My ears burn, and I go a little blind. Used to be, I was the Big Boy. *Big Boy*. Trudy called me that all the time. Now I see the curve of her head and hear the way she sings. Trudy is next door, so close I can almost smell her.

I can't see straight. I bang into the back door when I sneak out. I hold trees to keep from falling. I got no shoes on. I make it through the woods and finally hug this pine twenty feet from the car and stay out of sight. I want to tell her to shut up. *Don't go calling people names.* She's got her waitressing uniform on, but he's zipping it down, silver flashes in the lantern light.

"BIG BOY!" she says and steps out of it. She takes the rest off while he kicks his shoes into the shadows and pulls down his shorts.

Trudy lays back on the hood of his car, her knees in the air. "Watch out," he says, "the hood might still be hot."

"Shut up," she says. "Hot's right here." She laughs. I know that laugh. I still hear it sometimes when she ain't even around, one of those echoes that never really goes away.

He's standing up when he does it. Trudy beats out time on the fenders with her hands. They are both covered with sweat, their heads a few feet apart but neither one watching the other. She eyeballs the sky and starts singing along with the radio, her voice chopped up by his pushing. Sounds like she's got hiccups. He shakes his head once, and the sweat slings off and sparkles like fireworks when the light catches it.

"Big Boy," she says, and he keeps going on and on, reaching down and hooking his fingers through the grill so he can pull against her. I hear the shocks squeaking on his car. "Professor..." she sings out.

He starts screaming, but not at her. "NEIGHBOR!" he yells. "HEY, NEIGHBOR!" Motherfucker keeps up for another quarter hour, and I can hear him yelling even though I'm back in the trailer with a pillow over my head and all the windows closed up tight. The sound won't let me be.

I didn't think he had it in him.

?

The next morning, it's cloudy but nobody's calling for rain. Raymond pulls up with his blue lights on. They flash through the windows. He doesn't knock. He kicks at the bottom of the door.

"Wake up, you sorry shit-for-brains," he yells through the door. "And bring your goddamn toothbrush. You're going to jail."

"Get the fuck off my porch," I say because I need to sound serious.

"You're such a damn redneck. You're a fucking afterbirth."

I crack the door, and Raymond pushes through. He has his handcuffs out, and he slaps one of them on a wrist. "You got the right to be quiet and you got the right for me to kick your bony ass into next week, you shit stain." He cinches the other cuff before I can even open my mouth to ask what's going on. "Shut up," he says. "Don't even say a thing. You're moving out."

"The hell for?" I say, still confused.

"What do you think?" he says, steering me toward the door.

It's okay, though. I feel warm and happy. Raymond is hauling somebody off, but it isn't me, really. Most of the real me is laying balled up on the floor, thinking of ways to tell Trudy that I don't give a shit about her if she stays miserable, but the second she starts having a good time, I'm in love all over again. Even though she was double-humping the Professor on the hood of his car. Loved her *because* of that. It isn't a jealous thing. It's something that doesn't have a name. It's a different kind of confusion.

The real me, the one that doesn't give a flying fuck about Raymond, is thinking up ways to kill the Professor without a sound. I want time to think. I got no plans to talk. It is one of the first times in my whole life I decide to shut up. I have other things on my mind, and no handcuffs or no sheriff is going to clear my head.

"What you got to say for yourself?" Raymond finally asks me. He can't stand the quiet.

"About what? I haven't done a thing to Trudy. I haven't gone near that professor."

"Yeah, what about his dog?"

"Dog?"

"The college man's dog. The Professor's. I can't believe you. You're such a fuck up."

We are on the porch now. It is so cloudy out that it seems like evening or dawn. I take a breath and spit at the dirt. I haven't thought about that dog in days.

"I'm making you sit right in the wet spot." Raymond steers me again while we walk toward his police car.

"The hell you talking about? Wet spot? I haven't done a thing to that dog. He just ran off. He got lost. Maybe a snake bit him or one of those raccoons drowned him. Don't blame me because the dog got bored and left."

"I don't care about him leaving. What I care about is how he showed back up."

I wasn't expecting that.

"I know playing stupid comes easy for you, but give it up, okay? Just give it up," he says. "I can't believe you let that dog rot that way. Did you bury him and dig him up later? And you ruined my fucking back seat. Motherfucker was so full of maggots, I'll probably have maggots in my seat cushions forever. My squad car will probably get airborne from all the flies one day. And it'll be a miracle if the smell ever leaves. I been driving around with the windows open." Raymond's hands are down by his side, clenched into nervous fists.

I start laughing. Throw my head back and let it pour out of my mouth. Raymond tells me once to shut up, then he hits me. I feel my cheek pop inside my mouth, but I keep laughing. Even when Raymond stuffs me in the back seat and pushes my face into the wet, brown smell on the cushion, I keep laughing and keep laughing until it doesn't seem funny anymore, until I feel my breath backing up in my throat, and I start choking on my tongue. Raymond is in my ear.

"You puke and I'll make you lay in it," he whispers. I smile and make sure I keep it all down.

?

I stay in jail for two days. Raymond can't keep me any longer because he can't prove I killed the dog or put him in the police car. I don't know if they found the fish hook or not. Doesn't matter. A dog could pick up a hook anywhere along the river. Raymond can only get mad for as long as the law lets him. He won't even talk to me. I try to hitch a ride back out to the river, but there isn't one to be had, so I walk most of the morning and part of the afternoon. The tar on the road smells and shimmies from the heat.

When I round the curve on the river road, I see the deep tracks of heavy trucks. Cement trucks. The Professor is pouring the last footings for his house, leaning against a tree, watching a man in rubber boots aim the wet cement at the holes. He seems to know when I'm clear of the trees and in plain sight because he turns and smiles at me the whole way into my trailer. I flip him the bird, but it doesn't do a thing to his smile. There isn't a bit of fear on his teeth. He thinks he won. He is a new man. He thinks piling that stinking lump of a dog into Raymond's car made him the champion, thinks it was such a good trick. All it got me was a couple of days of free food and decent air conditioning.

They work most of the day, the cement man sweating through his dirty t-shirt and the Professor cutting a path back and forth between the wet footings and his water cooler. By the end of the afternoon, most of the foundation is poured and I'm settling in. I'm ready for the evening. My head buzzes like a ground hornet.

Trudy appears out of nowhere, a damn ghost, in the footprint of The Professor's house. She doesn't look toward my trailer. She's pretending I'm dead. She doesn't care one way or the other. I need to pee, but I'm too scared to walk outside. She's the only person in the world that makes me act this way.

The Professor takes off one shoe and sticks his foot in the wet cement. Trudy puts her hand in and giggles like she's touched something gross. They both walk down toward the river, to wash off the cement, I guess. I can't see that far. I lose them in the trees. I hope he steps on a water moccasin. I hope he steps on one, and she has to watch him do it. I wish as hard as I can for a snake. I pray for a snake with a mouth as big as an open Mason jar. But God doesn't listen to those kinds of prayers. You have to be your own kind of God sometimes. That's what I got out of church when I was a kid. You can wait on God to do shit, and you might die from boredom or being scared. Or you can take care of things yourself and let God figure out how to deal with the consequences. Most of the people walking around Hell are folks who got things done on their own when they were alive.

Be God my own self. That's what I do. I make it look like an accident. I've seen television shows. Slosh a little kerosene from the heater on the floor and on the mattress. Not much. I find a cigarette in the drawer, leftover from when Trudy used to be here. I take a couple long drags and lay it down on the mattress. Shouldn't have been smoking in bed. Bad boy, Big Boy. Everybody knows trailers go up like fat lighter wood.

The mattress is already smoking when I grab my clothes and throw them into a grocery bag. They haven't come back from the river yet. Probably swimming naked. They'll see it soon enough. Glowing like a big old giant lightning bug. As dry as it is everywhere, the whole woods will be going before long. I pray for wind. Fan those fucking flames. I might be God for a minute, but I'm not good enough to tell the wind what to do.

My truck starts right up, even though it hasn't been cranked in a few days. The radio works. I turn it up loud. They'll hear music, some kind of *thump-thump* down at the river. The trailer crackles, and the fire climbs up a pine that grows outside the kitchen. The last few feet, it just sucks right up into the limbs. The whole woods will be gone soon. The flames will stop at the river on one end and at the road on the other. I head my truck toward the highway, trying to decide which way to turn when I hit pavement. These woods won't be fit for a house for at least a couple of years. Black and ugly and burned out. I hope those raccoons get out okay, but I am not losing any sleep over it if they don't.

II

The Gable Massey Trio

Gable Massey Learns Some Greek

He cannot forget that fall.

Hollis took Gable to see a house she'd found, and he was not as immediately excited about it as she'd been. Gable was put off by the constant smell of bacon that percolated from the shag carpet in the rental house. The landlord blamed the odor on the former long-term tenants who ate greasy breakfasts every day of the week. He said Gable could rip out the carpets if he wanted to. Gable can recall wearing a protective mask when he pulled them up, soggy with age, and discovered the hardwoods beneath the padding, stained and sealed and unscratched. "See?" Hollis said as they stared at their shiny, perfect floors, almost afraid to set foot on them. "Don't you feel better now? I knew this was a good place."

Gable's memory grows spotty at this point. He knows there must have been some good months in the house before they got the news. Surely, they raked piles of leaves together. The sycamores in the front yard would have covered the lawn with leaves several times over. There may have been snow that winter, so perhaps he tugged Hollis through the new, slick neighborhood on his rusty childhood sled. He doesn't exactly recall bolting the backboard and the hoop into the eave above the driveway. Hollis certainly helped him put in the garden that April. He couldn't have planted it all by himself: the corn and okra and zucchini and pole beans. She would have still possessed some energy then, just on the other side of her first trimester. They must have walked to the garden and pulled weeds together. There were times like that, but he can't call them up now.

But he does remember that morning in the nursery with Hollis. Gable had just finished rolling the last wall. Only the window trim and the doorjamb remained. Two gallons of Canary Island Yellow. The previously dark-blue walls soaked up the yellow like a sponge. Hollis had picked out the color. The landlord gave them permission to turn the spare room into a place fit for a baby. That morning, Gable didn't want to look at Hollis. Instead, he stared out the window. July was nearly over, and the air hadn't shifted for days. The heat and mosquitoes were so thick, Gable couldn't even consider shooting basketball in the driveway.

Hollis hovered at the entrance of the room. She knew about the danger of paint fumes to pregnant women. She stood safely at the threshold to continue their conversation from the night before, a talk he'd fled for painting. She picked up the thread of it as if there had been no ten-hour hiatus. Gable had taped and painted walls through the night. He still wasn't sleepy.

"Looks good," she finally said. Then, "Listen, I just wanted you to understand. That's all."

Gable dipped a roller in the tray. "Understand, Hollis? Help me *understand* how you can consider that? Let me hear some rationale, okay? Do we even get to say hello to the baby? Maybe wave when they roll it away?" Gable paused and took a breath. The argument seemed inappropriate in a nursery. The words were too loud for the room. He looked through the window and across the yard toward his neighbor's studio and thought he saw Kevin weaving among his shelves of unglazed pots.

"I need to know it's an option. Just another option right now. I need options," she said.

"I'm painting a room. I'm making a place. You're looking for a way out. Isn't that interesting?" That night, while Gable had cut in the edges with a brush and rolled walls, he tried to understand Hollis's fear, and it always eluded him, disappearing into paint fumes.

Hollis pushed at the drop cloth with her toe. "Well, that's what *you* do. You muddle through. You carry things on your back. I don't muddle. I don't have the back for it." Hollis decided the conversation was over and was about to leave when the baby suddenly kicked. He saw the sharp unhappiness that creased her face, the same expression she owned each time the baby moved in her belly. Dr. Wallace told them it would be upsetting for Hollis to feel the baby squirm for space, knowing what they knew.

Gable let paint drip from his roller onto the hardwood. He could wipe it clean later. "We are not talking about options again."

He saw her face relax. He thought she might actually smile. But instead she said, "At some point, this isn't going to be a *we* thing. I'll be doing all the work." Hollis turned and padded down the hallway.

As far as Gable could recall, it was the first time they'd talked to each other that way, dishing out ultimatums, pointing out flaws. In the past, most of their arguments were small, silent affairs, minor standoffs. Hollis was right, and he knew it. He would take whatever came and learn to live with it, one way or the other. That was what Gable Massey did. Years earlier, he'd realized it required a lot less energy to take the punches instead of throwing them. Hollis was different. She was strong, but this scared her enough to create potential escape routes. Gable knew he should walk down the hall and wrap himself around her fear, but he couldn't make himself leave the baby's room until it was finished.

?

Earlier that month, before the worst of the summer heat, they had driven to see Dr. Wallace for a regularly scheduled appointment. Gable didn't like most doctors. He'd noticed over the years that most of them refused to look at patients when they talked. They distracted themselves with something else, like making notes in a file or probing a muscle with a thumb or nodding at the floor. Gable wondered why medical schools didn't offer a class in body language. He had come to appreciate Dr. Wallace, though. She had the roundest face Gable had ever seen on a human, the size and shape of a pie tin. Gable fought the urge to reach up and rearrange her features, to put her eyes closer together and her nose further toward her mouth. Hollis chose Dr. Wallace because she was a female obstetrician. In the few times the three of them had met, Gable felt as though Hollis and her doctor spoke a private language. They knew simple things he didn't.

After the ultrasound, Dr. Wallace asked if anyone in either of their families was unusually small. She wanted to know how tall their parents were. She posed the questions in an oh-by-the-way manner. The three of them sat close in a small examination room. Gable tried to focus on Dr. Wallace's round face, but it was a moving target. Her head swiveled on her shoulders, owl-like. To this day, Gable wonders why he didn't press Dr. Wallace at that moment, why he didn't ask her what she suspected. Maybe it didn't matter. Whatever was going to happen would happen. He would adjust.

Instead, Hollis was the one who wanted to know if a problem existed, and Dr. Wallace said she wasn't sure yet. "Just touching all the bases," she told them, smiling. Gable appreciated the sports reference. He understood it. Hollis appeared satisfied with the answer and glanced toward Gable, but he watched a blush rise from the collar of Dr. Wallace's lab coat, working its way up her neck, toward her face.

It must be awful, Gable thought, *to have your lies tipped off that way.*

?

Early one July evening, after a week of testing and consultations, of questions and half-answers, Dr. Wallace called just before dinner. Gable answered the phone, then started to call for Hollis. Dr. Wallace asked him to wait. "You can pass this on," she said. "That might be best." Gable felt his breath come quicker. He sat down on the floor in the hallway.

She went on to tell Gable that there were indeed problems. Things were happening that weren't normal. Measurements didn't add up. The legs were too short, the head too large. She used the word *mismatched*. She said *dwarfism* for the first time. She was going to refer them to someone who knew more about situations like this. "A geneticist," Dr. Wallace said. She gave them a place to be and a time to be there. She didn't allow Gable the space to begin a conversation. She said she would be monitoring things on her end, and he wasn't quite sure what that meant, but he was too scared to ask.

Gable rose to put the phone back in the cradle and turned to find Hollis standing over him. She held a spatula, pointing it at him. Dr. Wallace had done all the talking, so Hollis couldn't have heard much of a dialogue, but she was already crying. She must have known something, everything, from the look on his face. She waited for him to speak, but he couldn't think how to begin. A doctor called them and told them there were problems. *A doctor called them in their own home.* There was no good way to spin that.

Gable reached for Hollis and pulled her in. Between them, the spatula pressed into his chest. He felt her shudder and collapse a little, heard her corralling sounds in her throat. He couldn't form words. When she pushed away from him, he thought it was just to get room for her belly, but she wanted to break free. The spatula fell to the floor when Hollis turned down the hall. Gable started to follow, and she must have heard his footsteps. She closed the bathroom door before he got there.

"This," she said just loud enough to be heard, "is going to be so hard."

Gable knocked. He tried the knob. He put his ear to the door but didn't hear another sound. He held his breath to listen harder until the blood drummed in his ears. She must have been trying her best to be quiet, just like him.

He went back to the den, sat in a chair, and watched the light dissolve in the room. He imagined a baby with problems would cost them more money than they had. He guessed it would suck up large pieces of their future too. All kids did, but this would be different, he thought. It scared Gable how much he did not know. He closed his eyes until he heard Hollis walk by. He thought about asking her why she'd locked him out of the bathroom but decided against it. *Bad timing*, he thought.

Hollis walked faster than she should on the slick floors. *She still needs to take care of herself,* Gable thought. He followed her into the kitchen and watched her make a list of house projects on the back of an envelope. Next, she pulled out a drawer, the one filled with extra fuses and keys to locks they no longer owned, and began organizing it. She sorted through her coupon envelope and made a neat pile of the expired ones. Then, her energy evaporated. Hollis sighed and sank low into the chair.

"We'll figure it out," Gable said.

Hollis looked at him and cocked her head a little. Her hands rested on her belly. "Figure it out. That's almost funny," she said and pushed herself to standing. She stopped behind him and patted his shoulder like he was a friend from work or maybe a cousin. He felt her fingers linger a bit. He covered her hand with his and, for just a second, Gable thought they would be okay. He waited for her to say something, but Hollis pulled her hand free and headed down the hall toward the bedroom.

It was almost dark when Gable grabbed his basketball from the bucket in the garage and began to pound it against the concrete driveway. He dribbled under the basket and watched a pair of bats chasing mosquitoes from the treetops to the ground, diving in crazy circles. The cicadas hummed. The noises outside made him realize how quiet their house had become. He and

Hollis should be talking to one another; he knew that. But he didn't know how to begin a conversation with so much desperation lurking inside of it.

Gable started close, warming up. He flipped simple bank shots from the right and left, then made his way farther out. A film of sweat crept down his brow and into his eyes, and he used the bottom of his t-shirt to wipe his vision clear. The light was almost gone, the backboard and the hoop only silhouettes. He found the foul line, toed it, closed his eyes, and shot into the darkness. He heard the net snap as the ball fell through.

The things I'm good at don't make any difference now, Gable thought.

?

The geneticist was named Dr. Byrd, a large man whose white coat refused to button over his chest. His assistant, a young, doe-eyed woman, trailed behind him, often peeking around Dr. Byrd to get a better view of Hollis and Gable.

Dr. Byrd said he had studied their records carefully. He stretched the word *carefully* like a mantra, as if it would calm them. He explained that their baby was under the influence of some type of genetic dysplasia. His face brightened a bit, an eyebrow rose. "Did either of you take Greek in school?" he asked. "Very few people take Greek anymore, you know."

Gable and Hollis looked at each other and shook their heads. Dr. Byrd seemed pleased. "Dysplasia, roughly translated, means there is faulty development. And from the measurements we have here, the numbers don't coincide with normal development. The extremities, the skull, even the chest size...It's what we call a random gene mutation. Nobody's genetic fault, simply mere chance."

Gable thought Dr. Byrd said *displaced* instead of dysplasia, suggesting their baby was in the wrong location, a refugee in his wife's belly.

"The conundrum is this. Of the various types of dysplasia, many are non-life threatening. Problematic yes, but not fatal. In this case, we may be looking at achondroplasia. However, there is another variety, called thanatophoric dysplasia. Again, notice the Greek root." He waited to see if they could decipher the meaning.

"Well, thanatos is not positive. Frankly, it means... well, it involves death. Unfortunately, there is a possibility that when this baby is born, the lungs won't be strong enough to sustain and support regular breathing functions. I'm sorry." The assistant pursed her lips and nodded. Gable tried to find Hollis' hand without looking down. He grabbed her knee by accident, and she jumped in her seat. For three days, they had been imagining the worst. Now, they heard the sounds it made.

Dr. Byrd continued, "That's where we are genetically. One of two things, achondroplastic or thanatophoric. Okay, well." He sounded like a man trying to end a phone conversation. "Here is a sheaf of information

I copied for you. It might help you understand things better, be more informed."

Gable had never heard anyone use the word "sheaf" before in normal conversation. *That is probably Greek too*, he thought. *Everything important is Greek now.*

Dr. Byrd turned quickly; he was nimble for his size. He led his assistant to the door. She stopped in the doorway and turned to look at the two of them.

"I'm sorry," the assistant said just under her breath. "Sometimes, he gets caught up in the words."

?

Gable watched two camps develop, the achondroplastic and the thanatophoric. Dr. Byrd and his assistant and several of his geneticist colleagues at the clinic lined up behind thanatos. Dr. Wallace and a group of local neonatologists opted for achondros. Gable wondered if the achondros supporters were optimistic by nature and just couldn't help themselves.

Hollis and Gable had to talk to each camp several times, had to answer more questions, fill out more information forms. The baby always moved during the question-and-answer sessions. Gable could tell by watching Hollis' face and the way her hands suddenly reached for her belly. He began to wonder if there was a message in the movements. Did the baby react more during the thanatos questions? Or during the achondros ones? Did the baby have the answers?

He remembered mentioning this to Hollis, the idea that their baby was trying to give them a clue. She stared at him for a few seconds before she said, "If you think you are saying the right things, you should stop." He didn't respond. He watched her face. Hollis had gained thirty pounds, but her face was still as thin as always. All of the weight, all of the baby, was in front of her.

The quiet around them became heavier. Gable began to spend an hour or so each day driving around the neighborhood, noticing which houses were for sale. He imagined people moving into new places, better neighborhoods, happier lives. He didn't begrudge them the brightness of their futures, but he found himself wanting to stop and let them know that there were folks in the world who were afraid to look ahead anymore. At night, he and Hollis would sit in the same room and stare at the television, watching characters that said funny things, bringing on waves of recorded laughter. He wanted to laugh along every now and again, but he was afraid to put a dent in their silence.

Hollis did most of her talking on the telephone, calling her mother and her brothers to tell them about the baby. She called them every day, and every day she reminded them not to plan any trips until *she* knew what she was dealing with. When he listened to her halves of the conversations, he never heard Hollis mention his name.

Gable didn't call anyone. His family was so distant, especially since the death of his mother. He didn't worry about any of them paying surprise visits. He wrote his only cousin a note, letting him know they were expecting and would send photos when they had them.

Hollis said she planned to quit her vitamins and her exercise class. Gable couldn't blame her. She spent her mornings and afternoons reading books she brought back from the county library, most of them long, dense novels that she devoured in a couple of days. Sometimes, he wished his classes at the college would begin sooner. He was ready for something else to crowd his brain. He found things to do outside, like weed the garden or trim hedges or wash windows. Hollis wouldn't let him hang around inside the house. She said it bothered her, like someone constantly reading over her shoulder.

?

One evening, Hollis said she wanted Gable to help her walk to the garden, a request that took him by surprise. He couldn't remember the last time she'd tried the steep, uneven path between the two water oaks. Gable considered this a good sign. Since the meetings with Dr. Wallace, Hollis had stayed away from the garden. He'd been the only one wandering the rows of okra and squash, trying to fend off weeds and Japanese beetles.

"I'd like to see what is growing," she said as they walked out the back door. "It's been a while."

He held her elbow while they eased down the path. There had been little rain the past two weeks. They kicked up reddish dust with each short, careful step. He'd already placed a lawn chair by the edge of the corn. She groaned as she lowered herself. "Looks pretty good," she said, shading her eyes with her hand. "You must be watering a lot."

Gable began to talk fast, telling her how he'd been hitting it with the sprinklers in the morning just after breakfast, before the sun got too high. She said she hadn't noticed. Hollis fanned herself with both hands, then pulled her top away from her clammy chest to let in some air. "This wasn't such a good idea," Hollis said. "My feet are swelling. Jesus, it's humid."

Gable wasn't listening to her. Instead, he pointed out the new height on the okra plants and the way the squash vines spread kudzu-like across three or four rows. Yellow flowers had begun to form on the zucchini. He walked away from her, waving at the pole beans climbing up the strings he'd tied a month ago. He called out to her from the other side of the corn. "I put in some peppers over here, for salsa."

He wanted to bring her something he had grown, something that had ripened during the last few weeks. He wanted her to see that things were still going on in the world, plants were still growing, ground was still turning crusty. He wanted to make her feel better. He picked a double handful of tomatoes, the small Romas, and worked his way back through the rows to Hollis's chair. He carefully spilled the tomatoes into her lap. They rolled into a pile between her thighs, below her swollen belly. He made sure they stayed in one place. That's when he heard Hollis suck in a hard breath. Maybe the baby was moving.

But it was something else completely. Hollis looked up as he stood over her and drew another quick breath. Her eyes narrowed, and she wasn't staring in the sun. He asked, "What is it? Are you hurt?"

"I blame you," she said. "I know it's not fair, but I blame you."

Gable suddenly felt the thick heat and the dust. He hadn't given a thought to blame. From the tone of her voice, he knew Hollis wasn't angry when she said it. It was simply something she'd discovered, like a dime on the sidewalk.

From the second Dr. Byrd had told them about a random gene mutation, Gable had dismissed casting blame. It was one less thing to worry about. But Hollis hadn't. She wanted to point a finger, and Gable was the only one in sight. It didn't make sense, he knew, and it was ridiculous. But this random event, the mere chance Dr. Byrd mentioned, had put Hollis on a boat and him on an island, and now she was the one who seemed to be waving goodbye.

"Me?" he said as levelly as he could. She had pulled her collar down some, and Gable could see the blue veins that ran across her chest, markings that had appeared in the last couple of months.

"I've wanted somebody to blame, and you were here the whole time," she said. "The whole time, walking around the house, bouncing that goddamn basketball over and over. You were right here."

He opened his mouth to defend himself, but before he could speak, she began to throw the tomatoes at him, one at a time, like tiny, red bullets. She hit him in the chest and in the face. He didn't make a move to cover himself. The Romas were too small and too soft to do any real damage, but he felt every single one. She was so close, she couldn't miss. Hollis grunted each time she threw one. She didn't start to cry until she was out of ammunition. She struggled to lift herself out of the lawn chair. Gable couldn't decide whether to help or not.

"I can't do this," she said, rising to her feet. "And if I don't have to, I won't."

He thought she was talking about walking up the path, but he'd misunderstood her. She was halfway to the house before Gable realized he'd missed something in the translation, but still he stood there, the little tomatoes scattered randomly in the dirt at his feet, a code he couldn't possibly decipher.

?

Some mornings, Gable spent the early, coolest part of the day shooting jump shots and trying to come up with names for the baby. It was a game he'd created for himself. He would shoot until he made a basket, then count the number he made in a row after that. Whatever number he landed on, he would think of a name with that many letters. Most of the time, he sank only three or four in a row. Amy, Bob, Sam, Anna, Bill, or Jane.

Hollis had refused to let the doctors tell them the sex of the baby. And she refused to think about names. "I won't name a child that might not be here," she said. But Gable needed to give the baby something that wasn't Greek. He thought that no matter what happened, no matter whether thanatophoric or achondroplastic won, the baby deserved it. Once, he got on a roll and hit five in a row. He couldn't think of anything with five letters until it struck him. His name had five.

Late one afternoon, he picked the ripest tomatoes and a few handfuls of okra and carried the vegetables next door for his neighbor, the potter. Gable had been a regular visitor in Kevin's studio, an unpainted, tin-roof-over-particle-board building at the very back of his lot. Gable admired artists; he envied their ability to create something out of nothing. He'd even tried to be one himself, with his writing and his long-gone desire to make little films, but it had never panned out. He appreciated the fact that Kevin let him hang around while he sat at his wheel, spinning clay into shapes. What Kevin could do with his hands fascinated Gable, and he spent a couple of evenings a week sipping beer in the studio, watching and talking.

Kevin was in his usual uniform: raggedy shorts and a t-shirt, sandals. A dip of snuff crowded his lower lip. He glanced up from his wheel. "Ah, veggies. Helen will love those. Remember, I don't eat foods of color." Kevin rubbed his round belly, Buddha-like.

"The garden's too big for the two of us," Gable said.

"You getting closer to being a daddy?"

Gable touched one of the dull, unglazed pots. The studio was lined with wooden shelves, all of them sagging with pots, some glazed and fired, others waiting their turn in the heat. A thin coating of clay dust covered the cement floor. Gable left footprints where he walked. A small refrigerator hummed in the corner. Kevin got up from the wheel and retrieved a beer for himself, then offered one to Gable.

"Yeah, soon now," Gable said. Kevin enjoyed talking about babies, probably because his sons were grown and gone, one still in college, one graduated and working somewhere in Florida. Gable wondered if their births were smooth for Helen. For Kevin, too. Gable had told him nothing about dysplasia or the other Greek words. As far as Kevin knew, everything about their baby was normal, and Gable wanted to keep it that way. He wanted one place in the world where he wouldn't have to recite the latest chapter in the story. In Kevin's studio, he could drink cheap beer and talk about vegetables.

"Waiting can wear you down," Kevin said. He leaned over one of the half dozen tin trash cans that served as makeshift spittoons. "One of my boys came early, one late, so we had a little of both. You can't plan for anything with babies. Teddy, he was nine weeks early. He could have fit in a soup ladle, he was so damn tiny. But everything worked out. We've all gone through it."

If Hollis were there, Gable knew she would get angry and tell the potter that he couldn't possibly imagine what it was like, carrying something that might be making its last movements, its last attempts to get comfortable, before its lungs tried to handle the thick air of the real world. Hollis had begun to lay claim to all the disappointment available. He wondered if this new Hollis—the Hollis who was speaking less and less, the Hollis who wouldn't name a baby ahead of time—was a permanent resident next door, or if the old Hollis would return, the one who used to snort when she laughed too hard, who cracked her ankles in her sleep. Gable hadn't heard that cracking in months. He was smart enough to realize this was changing the both of them, but he spent nights awake, worried the alterations weren't temporary.

"Where's your radio?" Gable asked, wanting to steer the conversation away from babies and waiting. "The Braves are in St. Louis, I think."

"Cincinnati," Kevin said, correcting him. "It's on that back shelf. I moved it earlier today. The game doesn't start until seven thirty-five in Cincy. What's that, our time?" Kevin always knew where the Braves were and what time the first pitch would be thrown. When he got on the subject of baseball, Kevin worked the dip around his lower lip faster and spit more often. He loved to look ahead to fall and the World Series. Gable couldn't care less about the sport, but he knew how passionate Kevin was about it. All he had to do was nod and agree.

Kevin talked about the Braves' middle relievers and how they couldn't find the plate lately. Gable watched the afternoon fade outside the studio. He saw the dark outline of his house in the last of the light.

Kevin reached a crucial point with the clay on his wheel. He asked Gable to grab him another beer. Gable walked toward the fridge, leaving a new set of footprints on the floor. He retrieved only one, for Kevin. He needed to check on Hollis. He said goodbye and walked into the dark, ducking through the hole in the hedge. His basketball lay in the driveway. He walked to the foul line he'd spray painted on the concrete and toed it, bouncing the ball his usual three times. He hoped Hollis heard it, didn't care if she did. He made seven in a row in the darkness before he heard the clang of a missed shot.

A light suddenly came on somewhere in the house. The glow spread over the driveway. Seven. He tried to come up with a seven-letter name. The first thing that popped into his head was Seymour. *If I name a kid Seymour*, he thought, *he's liable to get the shit kicked out of him regularly on the playground.*

Then something else struck Gable. He was imagining his child alive, on the playground, having a fight with boys who teased him about his name. Gable felt good for the first time in a long time.

?

Late that July, Dr. Wallace called to suggest a date for induction. "Induction?" Hollis asked. Gable listened on the extension in the bedroom. She sounded scared. Dr. Wallace explained that because there was potential for complications, it would be best to induce labor, to have all the necessary equipment and people around. She said she wanted to control things as much as possible.

"And," she added, "I have a request from Dr. Byrd. He wants to be at the delivery, him and some of his people."

"What do you think about that?" Hollis asked.

"I don't like it," Gable answered.

"I wasn't asking you," Hollis said. Her voice echoed; Gable heard it in his ear and, simultaneously, from down the hall.

Dr. Wallace sighed. "It might actually be good to have him there. We'll do what we can to keep the delivery room calm for you. I don't know how many people we're dealing with here. Dr. Byrd, of course. Perhaps his assistant or someone else from their practice. Not many. If they start to get in the way, I'll get rid of them. I promise."

Someone else from Camp Thanatos, Gable thought as he hung up. He didn't think they had much of a choice. He guessed Dr. Wallace had already told the geneticists they could attend. But Gable let Hollis make the final call. He didn't want to argue with her.

That night, after Hollis went to bed, where she would spend hours hoping for sleep, Gable grabbed a flashlight from the kitchen drawer and walked to the garden, picking his way over the roots. The lawn chair was still at the edge of the rows. He sat in it and clicked off the light. On induction day, it would all change again, one way or the other. He could walk out of the hospital with more than he had ever bargained for. He might walk out more alone than ever. But at that moment, with the mosquitoes buzzing in his ears, he knew that he could never find his way back to the way things were before the news, before the house. The people he and Hollis used to be were shadows now.

He turned the flashlight back on and aimed the beam at the empty sky. The column of light seemed to go on forever toward the stars. He wanted to be mad at someone. Just like Hollis, he wanted someone to blame. With his empty hand, he swatted at his ears, then stopped for a second, glanced upward, and shot a bird at the sky. He raised his hand as high as he could, keeping his middle finger straight up. If God was up there, Gable hoped He was awake and saw the light.

?

Dr. Wallace and the geneticists and the neonatologists scheduled the induction for a Thursday in mid-September. Gable's garden still bloomed. New flowers on the squash, a fresh crop of tomatoes. Even the pole beans shot out more runners.

Gable broke a sweat carrying Hollis's things to the car. Mornings remained thick and warm. The doctors wanted to start the process just after seven, hoping for a baby around lunchtime. The geneticists and neonatologists had planned their day around Hollis's induction.

Even though it was warm, a breeze filtered in from the west. New weather was coming. Gable hoped for rain. He saw a plume of smoke escaping from behind the potter's studio. Kevin was up early to fire some pots in the Raku kiln out back.

Dr. Wallace met them at the hospital. Though she resided in the more optimistic achondroplasia camp, her lips were drawn together in a tight, nervous line. On the labor and delivery floor, she introduced the nurses who had just checked in for their shift, the ones who would help them through the induction. The word *induction* fascinated Gable. It sounded like a ceremony, like someone being admitted into a hall of fame.

Above the room where Hollis received the drip of the labor-inducing drug and where the nurses watched a monitor tape like a stock ticker, workers no one could see were doing loud hospital renovations. Gable heard nail guns firing compressed air and the whine of electric drills. At one point, a Vice President of Something at the hospital appeared and apologized for the noise. He winced every time the nail gun fired over their heads.

Just after the vice president left, Dr. Byrd and a stranger in a lab coat entered the room without knocking. "This is Dr. Tealander," he said. "I've brought him up to speed. I hope you don't mind him looking on."

"Do we have a choice?" Gable asked with all the edge he could muster.

Hollis shot him a look. "It's fine. Whatever, as long as it might help," she said. Gable hated the way his wife was grasping at anyone who walked in the door. He wished she would protest more, raise her voice a bit, but she was probably saving her energy for the delivery. He tried to smile at Hollis, but she lay on her back, staring at the ceiling, her face looking thinner than it had in weeks, her jaw set hard.

Dr. Tealander smiled at Hollis. "I wish you well," he told her. Gable decided Dr. Byrd had gone out and recruited for Team Thanatophoric.

Dr. Byrd examined the monitor tape. "Nothing much to this point," he said. "Maybe a small contraction, too small to feel. Insignificant." Gable wanted to ask Dr. Byrd how many *significant* contractions he'd personally experienced. Gable suddenly realized if the right opportunity presented itself, he could kill Dr. Byrd with just his hands.

Dr. Wallace said they might have a baby by three, but three o'clock came and floated toward four. They waited below the construction noises as the afternoon wore on. Gable peeked through the blinds at the dull, brick wall of the adjoining building. He couldn't find even a sliver of sky. They waited more, until the contractions arrived, or rather, the one drug-induced contraction, a lone, grinding, lightning-strike of pain that brought a wail from Hollis that Gable had never heard before. He tried to touch her, tried to ask her what he could do. The only sentence she managed to gasp behind her clinched teeth was familiar: "This is not a we thing."

He finally understood what she meant.

?

Two nurses arrived and wheeled Hollis to a delivery room. They handed Gable green scrubs and a mask and showed him where to change clothes. When he found his wife again, Dr. Wallace was leading her through another long contraction. In the background, gathered in a group against the far wall of the small room, Gable saw too many men, a half dozen or so, as well as Dr. Byrd's female assistant. He recognized her eyes over the top of her mask.

He reached his wife's side and took her hand. This time, she let him keep it. He needed to say something to help distract her from the pain. He began to talk about the garden. "It's almost over for the season," he said. "Only a few things left to pick." When the words left his mouth, he remembered the feeling of the Romas hitting his chest. That was where it became his fault, standing in the rows. He shouldn't have brought up the garden. Maybe Hollis wasn't even listening to him now. She squeezed her eyes shut. Gable wished she'd open them. He wanted to be sure they were still brown. Weeks and weeks had passed since he'd looked directly into those eyes.

Dr. Wallace nodded at him to continue, so he talked about his nights in the garden and how he sent light beams of messages into space, little bright SOSs. He didn't tell her about shooting the bird at God. Once, he thought he saw his wife smile at him, more of an echo than an expression, more of a reminder of how things used to be, how she used to curl her mouth at him when she was happy, in the days before they began translating Greek.

At five thirty-seven, their son appeared. He was small in the wrong places, which made him seem too big in others. Dr. Wallace didn't allow either of them to touch the baby. Gable felt heads craning behind him for a better look, strangers' breaths on his neck. He hated them all.

His son opened one eye as he floated by, one bright blue eye that tried to take in some of his new world. He couldn't tell if his son was breathing or not. He didn't make a sound, only gazed. The nurses took the baby to a table full of light.

Hollis began to cry. "You still have some work to do," Dr. Wallace told her from the end of the bed.

"Is he breathing?"

"Let's concentrate on this," Dr. Wallace said. "First things first."

"Has he taken a breath yet?" Gable asked for her.

His wife began to chant, "Make him breathe make him breathe make him breathe," while Dr. Wallace talked Hollis through the afterbirth. Gable shifted his attention from his wife to the table behind them, the one under the warm lights, where two nurses and a doctor he hadn't noticed before worked on his son. He saw Dr. Byrd slide near the table for a clearer view, his assistant lurking behind him. His wife changed her chant. She began to say over and over, "I don't hear him. I don't hear him making sounds. I don't hear him."

Gable told her not to worry yet, but even *he* didn't believe what he was saying. Dr. Byrd leaned into Dr. Tealander and whispered something to him. They nodded. So did the assistant. He couldn't detect the expressions under their sterile masks. The room grew silent. Dr. Wallace had run out of distractions. *The entire room just went numb*, Gable thought.

He scanned the room for a place to be sick. Warm saliva rose in the back of his throat. Dr. Byrd watched him and crossed his arms. At the bright table, nurses and the mystery doctor still worked on the baby, touching and calling out numbers that meant nothing to Gable. He took his wife's hand in both of his. She seemed helpless, lying on the bed, her eyes shut, chanting now to herself, a mumble or a prayer, her face the color of wet sand. He saw a trashcan and was about to release his wife's hand and run toward it when he heard his son scream into the lights. His wife stopped chanting and took a breath of her own. They all did. Everyone sighed.

But that was the only sound their son made. Gable looked toward the table. A tuft of dark hair lay matted on the crown of his baby's head. Both eyes squeezed shut. His mouth still and open, as if he wanted to draw just one more breath and tell his father one last thing.

?

Gable wandered. He walked in the opposite direction from labor and delivery, down hallways he had never seen. He pushed open doors for Authorized Personnel

Only, walked through housekeeping and maintenance areas. He thought about destroying something, about beating something important and expensive into tiny pieces. At one point, he rounded a corner and found the place where the new construction was taking place, where the nail gun had fired above them.

The workers were gone for the day, their tools lying where they'd left them. Gable moved quickly. He pulled every extension cord he could find from the wall sockets and coiled them all like lassos. A dozen or so, all different colors, bright orange and yellow and red, even a white one. Tomorrow, it would take hours before the workers found replacements and continued to bother the people below them who were trying to have babies. He threaded his arms through as many coils as he could carry and made his way to the rear of the hospital, toward the loading dock and the dumpsters.

On his way down a long corridor of tiles and fluorescent lights, a door opened and Dr. Byrd marched into the hall, trailed by his entourage of an assistant and a colleague. The doctor stopped in front of Gable, and he thought, *Go ahead. Ask me what I'm doing. Ask me if I know any Greek. I dare you to say something now.*

But Dr. Byrd kept his mouth closed. He only nodded at Gable and moved out of his way. The doctor didn't seem surprised to see him or the coils of extension cords. As Gable passed, the round-eyed assistant touched a place on his arm that wasn't covered by wire.

"Can you use some help?" she whispered low enough that only Gable could hear. By the time he decided to tell her no, she'd already moved on, and it didn't matter.

?

That night, Hollis told Gable to go home. She wanted to be by herself. "They asked me what to do with the body," she said. "How can people ask things like that?"

Gable said, "I should have thought about that."

"A little late. I really don't want to be near anyone now. Just go back to the house," she said.

It was after midnight when Gable pulled into his driveway. He turned off his headlights and noticed a glow from the potter's studio, the yellow-orange of dusty light bulbs, and an open door on a hot kiln. Kevin barely looked up as Gable walked in. He didn't seem surprised to have a visitor at that time of night. Kevin moved slowly, sliding a bare teapot into the door of the kiln with a pair of tongs. His face glistened. *He looks close to dropping it,* Gable thought. Kevin finally settled the pot deep in the heat and sealed the door.

"Hey, man," Kevin said, taking off his long gloves. "I saw y'all leaving this morning. You got some news?" He spat into one of the trash cans. The two of them moved away from the kiln, and Kevin grabbed a couple of beers as they passed the refrigerator. Gable slid some crates into the back door of the studio, so they could sit. A breeze sifted across his face, and he listened to the kiln throbbing behind them. He wondered how long before

Kevin had to check on the teapot. Gable was more tired than he thought. He shifted on the crate, trying to get comfortable. That was when he felt his eyes fill. For a second, he imagined Hollis was crying, too, back at the hospital. He hoped she wasn't trying to hear it again—that single, quick sound their son had made.

The potter studied him for a second, then said, "You can talk or not."

Gable Massey drew a long, deep breath of his own.

What Gable Massey Did After His Wife Left Him

He booked an appointment with an ear, nose, and throat specialist.

He couldn't recall if the hissing in his ears began before Hollis left him or immediately after. A chicken and egg dilemma. All he remembered is that the interference in his ears came on quickly. One morning, he woke up early and wondered why the television test pattern was making that monotonous hiss. Which was strange. Because the television wasn't on. That's what he told Dr. Gros.

"So it's not a *ringing*, per se?" the doctor asked. Gable thought ringing sounded more dangerous than hissing. He was convinced he had a sinister tumor bearing down on a crucial nerve or on one of those little bones that look like stirrups or hardware. (Gable Massey was not a hypochondriac, but when things didn't go away on their own, he started to worry. And, of course, he knew that fears come naturally with age.) Dr. Gros wore a little round mirror on the center of his forehead, attached by a wide headband decorated with several characters from Winnie the Pooh. The only hair on his head was a renegade swatch of orange fuzz that waved behind the mirror as if a breeze blew across the room.

"Hissing only. Like when you put a seashell to your ear." In the past few weeks, Gable had concocted a half dozen ways of describing the sound in his ears. It was definitely not ringing.

"I have conch shells like that in the garage at home. I do that ear thing sometimes just so I can get a vacation feeling. Strange, isn't it? Both ears, correct?" He paused, clearly enjoying his unexpected recollection. "Ah, well, what you have is tinnitus." This was the same diagnosis Gable's neighbor had offered. And she was an old woman who watched the neighborhood and picked up sticks in her yard, not a doctor. Tinnitus. Ringing in the ears—even though this wasn't ringing. It was hissing.

"Tinnitus." Gable repeated it aloud to let the doctor know he could still hear.

"Garden variety tinnitus. There are support groups and things for people who have it. Tinnitus really drives some people up the wall. They go mad. I suppose that's not something you want to hear right now, eh? Is the hissing keeping you awake at night?"

No, Gable told him. And that was the truth. Gable had been sleeping like a baby since Hollis left, which surprised and even delighted him a little. He would have predicted he'd lose sleep over her.

"Could it be the humidity?" Gable asked the doctor. In this part of the country, the humidity got blamed for everything from business failures to stillbirths. This summer had been particularly thick and clammy. Gable told someone just the other day that it was so humid, you could all but scoop up air in a Mason jar. At some point, Gable began to associate humidity with ear pressure and blamed the hissing on heavy air.

"It could be anything because no one knows what causes it. That's why they have support groups. Fear of the unknown." At the angle Dr. Gros stood above him, Gable saw his reflection in the doctor's tiny mirror. He thought, *I don't look tired. I look scared.*

"Tinnitus is usually a clue that you are starting to lose your hearing. Slowly lose it, I should say. Now, you seem a little young for all that to start, so we'll just test your hearing every six months or so. You can find those support groups on the web, I think." The way he said it, Gable could tell that Dr. Gros's hearing was fine, and he had no intention of ever having to deal with hissing in his ears.

Dr. Gros asked one last question as he reached for the door. "By the by, experienced any head trauma lately?"

He paid for a hooker.

Gable was surprised that he knew where to go. That place between the post office and the train station, where the street made a hard, unnatural left, sharp enough to slow any of the sporadic traffic that made the trip after dark. *I've become a cliché*, Gable thought. *A lonely, estranged white man with three twenties in his wallet.* When he graded student papers, he reserved his most violent, artistic circles for the trite language in their essays. One time, one of his young writers asked, "Why is it so awful to use something that everybody knows the meaning of?" Gable didn't have an answer. But he didn't retreat from his war on clichés. Even his own. Every man separated from his wife eventually thinks about a hooker, right?

He knew one thing for certain. He would not seek the benevolent prostitute. The hooker with a soft spot. The woman of ill repute with a heart of gold who could ferry Gable to the shores of salvation through the mere act of cuddling and listening to his story. A fifty-dollar hug. That is not what Gable Massey needed. *What I need*, he thought, *is a woman who dares you to flirt with death when she peels off her thong*. He wanted there to be the slim possibility that somewhere down the road, his penis would ultimately drop off like the nubby remnant of a baby's umbilical cord. This was Gable Massey's street-walker death wish.

He saw a woman leaning against the Amtrak sign, rubbing a stick of deodorant under one armpit. He wondered if this was proper prostitute etiquette. He slowed to make the sharp turn, lingering long enough to let the half dozen other ladies in slick boots and Salvation Army halter tops covey around his car. Deodorant Girl scratched her behind up and down on the sign. Gable wouldn't roll down his window until she looked his way. He waved at her to come to the car—a wave that was more like a plea. The other women leaned in toward every window of his car. Gable saw the sweat beads between their breasts. *The humidity*, he thought.

Her name was Lawson, and she smelled like a cosmetics counter. Six or seven scents covered and masked each other, in turn masking and covering something musky at her skin's surface. When she slid into the front seat of Gable's Volvo, she immediately reached between his legs. "Drive under the bridge, honey," she said. He told her he wanted to go to a hotel, and her price immediately jumped. Gable didn't flinch.

In the Econo Lodge, Lawson unzipped her boots and kicked them away. She wriggled out of a too-tight jean skirt and let Gable stare at the fact that she wore no panties.

"Do you have a heart of gold?" he asked her.

"Say what?" she called from the bathroom. She walked back in on her toes, tapping little dollops of hotel hand lotion into her palm, then spreading it on her bare shoulders.

"Are you the benevolent hooker?" Gable asked. He was seated on the bed, his palms resting on the tops of his thighs, which were still inside his pants.

"I got a pussy like thunder if that's what you mean." She started to turn back the velour spread on the mattress.

Gable stopped her. "Listen, my ears are hissing. I want you to do something for me."

"Ears?" she repeated.

He told her exactly what he wanted her to do. He asked her to whisper things into an ear, whisper so low that he almost couldn't hear. "Try to make me miss what you say," he said to Lawson.

"Whisper?" she asked.

"Kneel down here beside the bed. I'll lean my head over, then you whisper. We'll change to the other ear after a while." Gable lay on his back, his hands crossed on his chest.

"Something dirty?" she whispered.

"No, nothing like that," he told her. Gable was enjoying making up the rules as he went along.

Lawson went to her knees and put her lips close to Gable's ear. It took Gable by surprise when he recognized what she was doing. He knew the tune right away. She was singing her ABCs in a tiny, thin voice. She stumbled a bit early on and mangled the l-m-n-o-p section as well.

When she finished her zee, she paused for a moment, then reached across the bed and cupped Gable's crotch. He waited to feel something, a flutter, a rush, anything. The thought flickered across his mind that he had, indeed, paid for this woman, that he should try to get something memorable for his investment. Lawson moved her hand slightly upward, and Gable realized that he was utterly useless. He shut his eyes and shook his head. Lawson saw him, took her hand away, and whispered something so quietly that Gable imagined she could have been in another room. "You one fucked up white man."

I heard that, Gable thought, *loud and clear.*

He gave his wife a hint.

Gable Massey imagined that if he evolved into a subconscious, constant presence in Hollis's life, she would remember why she loved him once. Mere asking wouldn't bring her back. He had tried that. It needed to be subtle to the point of mystery. It needed to be osmosis. He didn't want to be seen so much as sensed. He didn't want to be an annoyance so much as a strange, sudden itch that arrived out of nowhere.

He began his nightly walks to Hollis's apartment after midnight. (It wasn't far, maybe ten or twelve blocks.) Hollis had forgotten the extra key to her Saturn station wagon, hanging on a finishing nail in the garage at the old house. Gable would hold the key in his hand the whole way to her place. In the parking lot of her apartment complex, he'd find the Saturn, unlock it, and crawl in the backseat, where he'd spend the entire night wrapped in the one blanket he brought with him.

Hollis and Gable used to take long trips during the first couple years of their marriage, trips that had no plan, no real purpose. They would leave in the middle of the night, picking a direction as they meandered to the edge of town. They would take turns driving. He loved the feeling of falling asleep while Hollis drove through the dark, wondering which state they'd be in when he woke up. And he loved watching Hollis sleep in the back seat when it was his turn to drive. He would angle the rearview mirror at her, catching shimmers of her reflection as they passed oncoming cars. He loved the quiet on those trips, the sounds of sleep.

Gable set the alarm on his wristwatch so that he'd be gone long before daylight. He thought about leaving her things, little remnants of their years. A photograph maybe, or a hair clip. Just something to slip into the crack in the seat. But Gable decided against it. That would violate his desire to be nothing more than a suggestion. The last thing Gable wanted to be at this point was too overt when he wasn't around.

Gable smiled when he imagined Hollis climbing behind the wheel in the mornings, looping her seatbelt across her chest and wondering why her Saturn always seemed to smell like her former husband.

Smells like Gable who is losing his hearing. Like Gable who is sleeping in cars. Like Gable who is helping a hooker with her ABCs.

He went to therapy.

Correction. Gable only told Hollis he went to therapy. During one of their sad, awkward talks in the days just after she'd left, Hollis told Gable she thought he should see someone.

"See someone," Gable echoed.

"A therapist. Someone you can talk to, who can help you figure yourself out. I sure don't know who you are anymore. I have this feeling you don't know either." Hollis was seeing a therapist. She had refused Gable's request to attend counseling as a couple. "I need to work on myself," she'd told him. "I don't have the energy to work on the both of us." She'd put it in terms of a favor. Do this favor. For me. See someone.

Gable thumbed through the phone book and looked under Counselors and Therapists. There were thirty-seven names. He knew Hollis was seeing a female therapist, so he decided on a male. Dr. Albert Carter.

Gable didn't have the money or the desire to actually call Dr. Carter and make an appointment. He just wanted a name. He needed a ghost doctor. This was his favor to Hollis. She didn't need to know that he never attended a session. And there was no way for her to find out. She couldn't check behind him. There were rules against that.

"Thank you," she said when Gable told her about securing the therapeutic services of one Dr. Albert Carter. "Did he help?"

"He was wonderful. A very quiet man. He sort of made me do all the talking. Getting my money's worth, I guess." Gable laughed, surprised at how much he enjoyed tampering with the truth. "He wanted to know the whole situation. He said he can understand how things got the way they were. The way they are, I mean."

Hollis stared at Gable and cocked her head slightly. "He said that?"

"Yes. He's very insightful. I told him how you felt you didn't belong in our house anymore, you know, that day at the kitchen sink with the crying and everything, and he said that maybe there was a coming together of things, timing he guessed, or actually bad timing that pushed us around a little. And of course, the baby." Gable rushed on, not wanting that memory to linger.

"But—and here's what I thought was so smart of him—he said that those sorts of things can be overcome if both people are willing to try, you know, give it a shot together and, of course, if the two people involved aren't arguing about anything in particular, if it's, well, like too abstract to figure out." Gable paused, realizing that he was talking faster and longer than normal. Hollis continued to stare at him as if he was speaking in tongues. "I really liked him," Gable offered up into the silence.

"So, where's his office?" she asked.

"That medical mall. Over by the hospital."

Hollis nodded. "Really? Did you make another appointment?"

"Next week. Early on."

"Thank you. I really appreciate you taking the time to find a therapist." Hollis smiled at him for the first time in weeks.

"Dr. Carter thinks I'll make progress. He said to be sure and tell you that."

Hollis's brow furrowed. "He said to tell me?"

Careful, Gable thought. *Careful.*

"Actually, he said I should feel free to discuss any of our sessions with you. Whatever I thought might help things, I should mention it. That's what he said."

"Gable, therapy is for your benefit. It's not going to bring me back." When Hollis said something she'd rehearsed, she had a habit of biting her lower lip. "We are a little beyond that."

"Dr. Carter told me you might say something like that," Gable answered. Hollis was still biting her lip when she turned away.

He sorted mail in the sunroom.

When Gable came home from school in the afternoons, he liked to drink a beer and go through his mail in the small room at the side of the house. He still received a great deal of Hollis's stuff, both the important things and the junk. He made quick decisions about which envelopes were important enough to pass onto her. It didn't bother him to sort her mail. It felt useful, like he was helping.

One afternoon, a large envelope arrived, addressed to Gable. It came from the law firm of Dooley, Miller, and Henry. Inside, a handwritten note on formal Dooley, Miller, and Henry letterhead said,

> *Per Mrs. Massey's request, we are forwarding a copy of this document for your review. Please have your attorney note any corrections or suggestions and return to us immediately.*

Gable couldn't make out the signature.

It was the first time he'd seen his life on paper, his possessions divided and subdivided, his history with Hollis broken into neat, formal paragraphs. He finished his beer, got another, and read the document again. Hollis had mentioned days ago—actually on the same day that he first reported on his therapy session with Dr. Carter—that she was moving ahead with things. *And this is what movement feels like*, Gable decided.

In the document, Hollis' lawyer listed several specific objects in the house that should be considered hers and not marital property to be divided. Those were the things that Gable brought into the sunroom and destroyed. A pot thrown by an artist in North Carolina. Crystal champagne flutes from Hollis's grandmother. An etching from an art gallery in Atlanta. *Et cetera*.

Each time he broke or ripped something, Gable tried to come up with a clever line or witty sendoff, the kind of line he imagined a suave actor like Cary Grant might say in a movie. So when he slung the pot on the floor, he said, "Not quite the vessel it used to be." When the champagne flutes exploded on the tiles, he said, "Not a good year for champagne anyway."

He brought the broom from the laundry room, swept up the pieces he could find, and poured them into a large cardboard box. Then, he washed out the empty beer cans and tossed them in the box as well, just to hear the sound they made.

He slowed down on the curve.

Even though it was long after midnight, Lawson was still out, holding up the Amtrak sign with her backside again, digging through her pocketbook when he waved to her. She must have told the other girls about Gable; none of them tried to approach the car.

She climbed in and leaned over, bit his earlobe, and said, "Hey, Whisper Man." Then, she noticed the cloth wrapped around his hand. "What? You bleeding?"

"I cut myself this evening. On a champagne glass. It's nothing." When she climbed in, he pulled a U-turn and drove toward the other side of town.

"You bring me any?" Lawson said.

He broke a sweat.

Gable spread the blanket in the back seat of Hollis's Saturn as neatly as he could manage in the dark and motioned for Lawson to get in. "I take it we ain't just whispering tonight," she said as she rolled her hips into the air and slid the jean skirt down her legs.

Gable closed the car door quietly and took a deep, deep breath. He smelled Lawson's fresh deodorant and the several different cheap perfumes and colognes fighting to do their mutual masking and covering. Tonight, she was chewing gum too. One of those happy smells. *Spearmint*, he thought.

Lawson asked him to open a window and let some air in, said it was too hot to be fucking in a car with the windows up. He didn't answer and didn't reach for the buttons for the window, just pushed himself inside her. Lawson began to recite her ABCs slowly, then began to moan in rhythm with Gable's movements, growing louder with each beat. He didn't notice the noise, didn't hear a thing. Gable had closed his eyes and was busy imagining what Hollis would think the next morning when she slid in behind the wheel. He wished he could be there to see the way her nose crinkled, to see the confusion on her face as she wondered what that smell was. She would try to pinpoint the odor, the smell of two bodies, wondering if it was actually her. *Is it just me?* He wished he could hear what she had to say.

Gable opened his eyes and looked down at Lawson. He realized he was dripping sweat onto her from his forehead and the tip of his nose. Her mouth was open, but he couldn't make out what she was yelling. The buzzing in his ears drowned out any other sound.

Lawson reached up and pushed Gable's chin toward his shoulder. She pointed at the slightly fogged window. Gable began to turn as the beam from the flashlight struck his face. Muffled voices, several of them, filled the empty spaces outside of the car. One of them, he recognized. "Gable?" Hollis said, "is that you? Gable, what is wrong with you?"

He felt Lawson's lips on his ear. "Sounds like somebody here knows you," she whispered, and suddenly, Gable heard everything clearly.

Gable Massey Makes a Movie

When Gable Massey heard the ambulance scream up to the Randalls' speckled brick house one hot, late afternoon, he didn't know his 'cross-the-street neighbor had just died for a few minutes. Gable glanced down the street to see who else stood on their porches, watching. Sirens were rare in his neighborhood, and they always brought the people out, eager to witness a commotion that might result in a new house going on the market. Gable wondered if the neighbors had been eyeing his house in the year and a half since Hollis left, waiting for him to plant a for-sale-by-owner sign in the grass and move on.

The EMS people carted out Betty Randall, just back from the dead. She was a bony, bird-like woman who spent a great many of her waking hours roaming her yard, digging and pulling and piling, directing her husband on his riding mower, firing spurts of Roundup at weeds that crept through the cracks in their cement driveway. Gable had watched Betty in the hottest afternoons of the summer, hacking at dandelions with her hoe, the sun blaring off the hair that she re-dyed more or less the same shade of flame red every few months.

He grabbed his small digital video camera and crossed the street into the Randalls' yard. It was familiar territory. Two or three afternoons a week in the summers, he saw Mrs. Randall struggling stiff-legged up the gentle slope of her front yard, tugging a tarp loaded with branches or weeds, taking only a step or two before she bent at the waist to catch her runaway breath. She seemed to have an endless supply of yard trash. Whenever he saw her struggling, Gable dropped what he happened to be doing—stopped pushing the mower or washing the car or weeding the beds—and trotted across the street to pull the tarp to the curb for her, scared she might collapse if he didn't help.

It had become a ritual between the two of them. Betty never really thanked him for dragging her things up the hill. Instead, she would comment on Gable's yard. Something like, "Yours is looking good too, neighbor." That is, until Hollis left. Since then, Betty would wag a finger at his face and say, "Odd that your wife up and left."

It didn't bother Gable that Betty brought up his ex-wife. He was proud that in the space of eighteen months, he had finally gotten to the point where Hollis was only an occasional memory and not a constant rapping on his brain.

Betty Randall would say, "How can a woman leave such a nice house and nice yard? Where is she now? An apartment? Who would leave this for an apartment? There are plenty of women who would love a house in this neighborhood." She waved in the general direction of Gable's property. He watched the loose skin sway hammock-like on the back of her arm. When he didn't answer, she would close the conversation with, "Things happen between people, neighbor."

The first time or two she mentioned Hollis's leaving, Gable tried to explain what had happened. He looked Betty right in the eyes and told her about Hollis's needs. He found himself using versions of the word *need* a great deal, more than he would have liked. *She needed to find herself. She needed space.* He left out the parts about the other man she needed.

Gable didn't want to complicate things for Betty. He kept it simple. As he talked, he watched Betty's eyes and noticed a glaze wash over them. She didn't really care. She'd come back with something like, "Did she take the Christmas decorations? You two had lovely Christmas decorations." Gable had learned to pull the tarp to the curb and leave Betty's questions unanswered.

The day Betty Randall died, Gable met one of the EMS workers in the driveway, a tiny woman who, from a distance, looked as though she couldn't lift a sack of sugar. Up close, he could see she was solid and strong. "I'm the neighbor from across the street," he said. "This looks bad."

"I can't talk now," she answered quickly and continued to walk without glancing at him. Then, as if she hadn't listened to herself, she gave him all the details he needed. "Older white female was shocked, electrocuted basically, and blown across the room. Twenty feet or so by my count. Her hip is shattered, I think. She was basically dead for a few minutes. Deader than a doornail."

Gable filmed her, but the EMS worker didn't know it. His digital camera was so tiny, he could cradle it in his palm, hit the play button with his thumb, and aim it from his thigh at the EMS person. She couldn't possibly see the small red dot at that angle. Gable liked to film people who might not talk if they knew a camera was trained on them. Sometimes interesting people clammed up in front of a camera. Gable wasn't trying to blackmail people. He just wanted folks to be themselves.

"My god. Is she going to be okay? What about her husband?" Gable asked. "Should I help with Fred?"

"A little woozy, shaken up. He'd already resuscitated her when we arrived. Unbelievable. We're worried about shock for the both of them. The other kind of shock, I mean." She almost smiled at her joke, then reached into the back of the ambulance, grabbed a short stack of blankets, and trotted toward the basement without saying another word.

As she left, Gable put the camera to his eye and filmed her quick exit around the corner of the house, giving the whole scene a nice, full ending. He hoped he had aimed right, hoped he got her saying "deader than a doornail" on camera. *That wasn't the kind of thing an EMS person would say if she knew a camera was on*, Gable thought.

He waited until the group emerged from the basement, his camera running. Betty curled on her side on a stretcher, moaning slightly. Her eyes blinked open. Gable wasn't surprised she'd come back from the dead. He couldn't imagine anything having the gall to kill Betty Randall. The clothes that peeked out from beneath the sheet were brown with wet, muddy stains. He thought Betty caught a glimpse of him standing at the edge of her driveway, and, for a moment, he was scared she might ask him again why his wife abandoned such a nice house and nice Christmas decorations.

Fred Randall didn't see Gable at first. His head was down; he was concentrating on the uneven pavement between the aluminum legs of his walker, an official EMS blanket draped over his shoulders. It reminded Gable of those sad black-and-white portraits of broken-down football players.

But Fred Randall wasn't in shock. He was drunk. Gable wondered why the EMS people didn't spot the signs. He would have imagined being observant was part of their job description. Fred wavered on the asphalt, grabbing the rubber hand grips, steadying himself as if he were battling a breeze no one else could feel. His eyes were washed out and red, like they always were when he showed up at Gable's door in the late afternoon.

When Fred finally saw Gable, he turned his head slightly, smiled, and winked. Gable glanced at his hip and made sure the red light was shining. He hoped he got that shot, too. He would have never expected a wink at a time like that. The little, wonderful surprises the world tossed out—those were the things keeping Gable from feeling completely abandoned. With his camera, he could be the quiet, unofficial collector of the unexpected. He wanted that job. Having the lens open was his way of avoiding being completely blindsided by anything. Like drunk neighbors who winked. Or wives who moved out of nice houses.

?

For the past seven or eight months, Gable had worked sporadically on a movie about love. He didn't set out to make a film about such a complicated, often-dissected subject. After Hollis left, he bought the digital camera as a way to stop being so angry at her. He needed something else to occupy his time and his head. Gable found that if he wasn't busy when he was at home, he ended up on his back on the couch in the sunroom, staring at the arrangement of water stains on the ceiling, envisioning the runaway bus Hollis might walk in front of or the embarrassing diseases she might catch from her new boyfriend. He suspected his anger wasn't healthy.

He wanted to buy an 8mm camera, like the one his father brought home the summer Gable was seven or so. Gable always loved the fact that the 8mm camera had no audio; once the film was developed, the characters projected onto a white sheet in the family room jumped around and opened their mouths, but nothing came out. Gable remembered making up dialogue for his aunts and uncles and cousins who appeared on the sheet. These days, it was hard to find 8mm film, much less a place to process it. Ultimately, Gable opted for the digital video camera, complete with a small, wireless microphone setup.

When the camera arrived, he decided he would film whatever caught his eye and piece the images together into something that made sense. The more unexpected, the better. Or maybe he would be the neighborhood surrealist and film things only *he* could identify. Anything to keep him off that couch.

When he sat at his computer and started downloading and cataloging the clips he shot—a stray cat cleaning itself in the street, close-ups of mosquitoes landing on his arm and biting him, water gushing out of a downspout during a thunderstorm—he realized he was boring himself. That's when Gable decided to make a movie about the one thing in the world that confused him most at the moment. He couldn't decide if he still loved Hollis, couldn't really remember what he meant when he used to tell her he loved her. Before she left, Hollis told Gable that she needed the passion every day. Not just the basic off-the-shelf passion, but *the* passion. Now, a year down the road, Gable thought a lot about passion and love but wasn't sure if he knew the difference between the two.

He would make a love movie. He would ask people he knew to sit on the plaid couch in his living room—the one Hollis left behind—and talk about, well, about whatever they wanted to. But Gable would eventually steer them to the topic of love. The effects of love. The damage of love. Proof of love.

Something about love.

?

What Gable discovered quickly: no one wanted to talk about love. Maybe the idea of talking to a camera scared them. Or maybe they didn't have much to say about love. The neighbors, some teachers from his school, even a distant relative in town all turned him down. The few neighbors who agreed to sit in front of the camera were content to tell sentimental stories or to say things like "love is commitment," phrases Gable had heard a hundred times in movies or read in books. Or they talked about a first love in the seventh grade or how much they loved their father or mother or a pet Santa brought them one Christmas. Although he didn't let them see it, Gable was disappointed. He wanted surprises. Only a few even made eye contact with the camera as they laughed and tap danced around Gable's requests to dig deeper into the subject of love.

He tried to make light of it. "C'mon," he would say, "forget about the camera. How did you know you were in love the first time? Could you fall in love with someone new, right now? Is it too late for love? What do you think?" His interrogations didn't help at all.

Gable finally met someone more than willing to talk about her version of love, met her during a barbeque at the neighborhood pool. Candles floated on the surface of the water that night. A string of paper lanterns wove through the chain link fence between the parking lot and the pool deck. Gable spent most of his time near the makeshift tiki bar, huddled with a half dozen other people.

Laurie was new to the neighborhood, divorced for a couple of years. She had two small children, a boy and a girl, and when she discovered Gable was a teacher, she asked question after question about the quality of the schools and the availability of carpools for Wednesdays and Fridays. Laurie wondered about the average test scores in the nearest elementary school. Gable told her he was a writing instructor at the local college, and he didn't have any children himself and didn't know about test scores. "Truth be told," he said, "I don't have a wife either." *A clever remark*, he thought.

The fact that Gable lacked answers didn't seem to disappoint Laurie. She never stopped smiling. He stared at the surface of the water, imagining what would happen when the candles burned down to their little rafts. He wondered if he would be able to hear the sizzle. Laurie appeared comfortable with the long pauses in their conversations, using the time to sip on her beer. Gable noticed that his friends had all drifted away, leaving the two of them beside the tiki bar. He thought he detected something else going on aside from the information gathering. Gable couldn't remember the last time he tried to read the signs. He started to ask if she knew about the fate of the candles. He decided against it. When she drained her plastic cup, she didn't move to refill it. Breaking the silence, Gable told her about his movie project and his difficulty finding the right kind of subjects to face the camera. Laurie didn't blink. She immediately offered to sit on his couch and talk about love, or, as she said, "the recent lack thereof."

After the barbeque had been taken away and one of the party committee members retrieved the floating candles with the lifeguard's shepherd's crook, Laurie and Gable walked around the corner to his house. He wondered if anyone watched him take a woman home. He liked his neighborhood at night. It felt protected by the dark. The smell of grass mown that afternoon lingered in the sluggish, summer air. Teenagers parked their cars at the curb instead of sharing the driveway with their parents. A cat ran across the street when Gable and Laurie walked too close to its hiding place in the storm drain. The Randalls were already asleep. Gable figured they were too old to stay up late, but in the other houses, windows bloomed with light. Laurie talked the entire way to his house, punching Gable's shoulder when she thought she'd said something funny.

At his house, Gable warned her about the lights he used with the camera. "They tend to intimidate people sometimes," he said.

"Not a problem here," she called from the kitchen. Laurie made herself a drink from the vodka in Gable's freezer. She found it without asking, as if she'd known there would be a bottle waiting for her.

After Laurie settled on the couch and Gable pinned the microphone to her collar, he studied her through the viewfinder. He hit the zoom function and went to an extreme close-up of her face. She was very angular, very sharp-featured. Her cheekbones were constantly tense, as if she were clenching her back teeth, her face browned by hours at the pool. A tiny mole floated under one eye. He hadn't noticed it at the party. Gable made sure the focus was set for automatic, backed off the close-up, checked the viewfinder, then put his headphones on. Laurie set down her drink heavily on the table beside the couch and began to peel her shirt off, still staring directly at the camera when her head reappeared from beneath the cloth. She was wearing a sports bra and pulled that off as well. The sound of rustling clothes crackled in Gable's headphones. She found her glass without looking away from the camera and killed the last of the vodka.

Gable didn't know what to do. He tried to finger the power button on the camera just to shut everything down but accidentally hit the manual adjustment, and the focus went soft. He panicked. He couldn't decide whether to continue looking through the viewfinder or peer around the camera. He suddenly didn't feel safe behind the tripod. But he wanted a closer look. It had been months since he'd seen a woman's body. There had been others since Hollis, most of them based on hasty decisions that involved an odd sort of revenge or too much beer or a combination of both. Lately, however, there had been nothing, no one. He hadn't worked up the energy. Now, a woman sat on his couch without her shirt, willing to talk about love.

"How's it look, Mr. Spielberg?" Laurie asked, fishing for an ice cube with her fingers.

"Well, I mean, good, of course," Gable stammered, sliding his head from around the camera, "but I'm not sure this is what I was talking about when I told you about the movie. I don't want you to think I..." Gable didn't know how to finish his sentence.

"Oh relax," she said, tugging on the zipper of her jeans. "You want to know about love? Here's what I've learned about love: keep your mouth shut and be flexible at all times. End of story." She popped an ice cube in her mouth and crushed it with her back teeth.

Gable didn't understand what she meant. He waited for her to go on, but she was busy with her pants. Maybe she did know about love. Maybe she could show him about *the* passion. She could define or redefine things for him. He stared through the viewfinder again and panned down slightly. Laurie stood and pulled off her pants, and he noticed how muscular her calves were. And her arms were not bunched like a weightlifter's but were naturally tight and toned. Her toenails were bright red. Laurie was comfortable under the lights, without clothes. Gable noticed the horizontal scar low on her belly. He zoomed in a little. Laurie caught him pointing the camera in that direction, and she traced the scar tissue with her finger. "From baby number one," she said, smiling. "He took the quick exit."

Gable thought about Hollis, how she always controlled the atmosphere when they made love. Lights had to be off, doors had to be closed, blinds had to be lowered. He wasn't allowed to wear his wristwatch during sex. It felt like sex during a lockdown. He wondered why he couldn't remember any of the good times, times when he and Hollis held hands or laughed out loud. She had a laugh too big for her body. Maybe more of those memories would return one day, revive themselves in his brain.

Gable reached for the switch on the light nearest the camera. It dimmed quickly. Laurie walked toward him, jiggling the ice in her empty glass. Gable took off his headphones.

"I thought we were doing an interview," she said and turned the light back on. Gable happened to glance directly at the bulb when it re-fired, and it blinded him for a second. When his sight cleared, Laurie was back on the couch. "Let's talk," she said. And that was what she did for the next hour—stare into Gable's camera and talk about the things she loved. She talked and Gable listened. That was all.

The next weekend, when she saw him standing near the concession stand at the pool, Laurie walked over and shoved Gable on the shoulder like he was a teammate of some kind. She smiled and said, "How's the movie coming, Mr. Spielberg? Don't forget to invite me to the premiere."

She spun and walked away before Gable could answer. He watched her calves. He wanted to tell her he had shelved the movie idea that night, shelved it the moment she left with her clothes on, carrying what remained of Gable's vodka. He didn't give up because of anything Laurie said as she lay back on the couch, her skin glistening a bit from the heat of the lights. It wasn't her fault he halted his amateur production. He just realized he might not be all that interested in what he discovered. He didn't want to make a movie that bored anyone, especially him.

?

A week or so later, Betty Randall died and was brought back to life by her husband. That's when Gable decided to get the love movie going again. This time, he would change the direction a bit. He would concentrate on Betty and Fred. He would get them to talk in detail about the experience in the basement. Gable was sure what he'd been searching for with his little movie was a symbolic act that validated the damn emotion, that made love real.

Screw sappy stories and keeping your mouth shut and passion and flexibility and whatnot, Gable thought. *Finding your wife dead and blowing air into her lungs. Bringing her back from the dead. Now that was pure love.*

Gable imagined Hollis would have never needed a new apartment and new passions if he had only saved her life at some point. Perhaps the excuses she'd given him—about the need for space and time and *the passion*—would have been meaningless if he had, at some point, filled her empty lungs or jarred loose a piece of sirloin lodged in her windpipe. But Hollis never came close to dying, never came close to giving him the chance to perform a miracle. The only thing Hollis ever needed saving from was, apparently, Gable.

He knew Fred would wander across the street once Betty was settled in the hospital. Before Betty's accident, he showed up at Gable's door two or three afternoons a week just after five o'clock, offering up his own brand of chitchat until Gable asked if he wanted a beer.

"Let *me* get one for us," was Fred's normal response. "I know where you keep 'em. You're not making me drink alone, are you?" Because Fred used a walker everywhere he went, Gable felt guilty that his neighbor retrieved the beers. But Fred seemed happy taking care of himself, content that he earned his free beer by dragging the walker across Gable's house.

Fred loved to hold court, to talk about the most nothing of things. He never needed a prompt to begin a story. He wouldn't be intimidated speaking to a live camera. Fred once told Gable that he had thankfully reached the age where he could say whatever popped into his head and not give a shit about who heard him. Gable couldn't believe he hadn't thought of filming Fred before.

On Thursday, Fred hobbled into Gable's kitchen and gave an update on his wife's progress. She was recovering from a completely shattered hip that had been replaced, as well as several broken ribs. In the midst of his story, Fred cut his eyes in the general direction of the refrigerator, and Gable told him to go ahead. Fred shoved the two cans in the front pockets of his oversize khaki pants and headed back into the den with his walker.

Gable noticed how much thinner Fred looked, like he'd been worrying too much and eating too little. When Fred finished the long and meandering details about his wife's hospitalization, Gable told him he had a couple of steaks he could throw on the grill. Fred said he'd rather have another beer. He rose from the chair and bumped his way back into the kitchen.

After several more rounds, Gable worried his beer supply might be growing low. He had a twelve pack in the garage, but it was hot. "Here's what they figure," Fred said. "Betty must've walked into the basement without seeing she was standing in an inch or so of water. Basement leaks like a sumbitch. Sump pump went out years ago. Never got it fixed. You know those bedroom shoes Betty wears all the time? Maybe not. Anyway, the water soaked through the bottom of them, they think. Well, she goes across the floor and throws that light switch at the far end of the room, the one without a switch plate near the stairwell, so she can see what she's doing and what it was is what they call an arc."

With his free hand, the one that wasn't holding a beer can, Fred waved at the air. He reminded Gable of an orchestra conductor. "The electricity jumped out of the light switch into her thumb and scorched it all to hell and back. The worst of it was, the shock blew Betty across the room to the doorway. That's where she landed and died for a few minutes 'til I showed up."

Fred stopped for a sip. He was so nonchalant that his wife was, for all intents and purposes, gone at one point. Gable started to ask Fred how he felt when he found Betty, but he caught himself. He wanted the answer on camera, not floating around in the air. Right then, he pitched his idea to Fred. He told him he was filming people talking about their relationships. He spoke slowly because he was trying to decide what to leave out. He didn't use the word *love*. He didn't tell Fred about Laurie and the camera. He told Fred everything he thought necessary to get him to sit down on the couch and relate the Betty story. "I'm just letting people talk about somebody important to them and what keeps them together," Gable said.

"Got yourself a little camera and trying to figure out the ways of the world, eh?" Fred said, breaking into a smile.

"I suppose," Gable answered. Once he read an interview with a famous director who said that every movie he ever made was ultimately a movie about himself. Gable hoped he wasn't that transparent to Fred.

"Let me grab an extra beer. I'll talk to your camera. I got plenty to say." Fred aimed his walker toward the kitchen, and Gable almost sprinted to the spare room to set up the lights.

❓

He used a standard three-point lighting scheme he'd learned years ago from a filmmaking handbook—a softbox for the face, a little fill in the background, maybe a touch of reflection off a white card under the chin. Gable didn't want the camera to pick up the shadows beneath Fred's eyes, dark pockets that had become more pronounced since Betty's accident.

Fred watched Gable scurry around. "Who's gonna see this beside you?" he said.

"Maybe no one. I don't know." Gable wished he had better answers.

He sat Fred on a stool in front of a beige wall free of photos or shelves. He clipped a tiny wireless lavalier microphone to Fred's collar and put an extra one on himself so the questions he asked would be nice and clear on the footage as well. He hit the button, and the camera powered up.

"I'm ready," Fred said, staring at the lens. "You ready?"

"Okay, you already told me how Betty got hurt. The arc," Gable said.

"Hurt? Son, she wasn't hurt when I found her. She was dead. There's a difference." He took a long pull on his beer. Gable watched through the viewfinder. It was the most real-looking thing he'd filmed since he bought the camera, the sight of Fred turning up a beer can just after pronouncing his wife dead.

Gable asked, "You and Betty have been married how long?"

"She was dead and blocking the door, and I couldn't push it open."

"Okay, well," Gable said, then thought, *I'll try something else.* The audio levels sounded fine in his headphones. "When did you know you loved her?"

"I hollered at her to get out of the way, dammit," Fred said. "I'd been cutting the grass. She ain't never happy until the grass looks like a goddamn golf course."

"Okay, we can talk about the accident first."

Fred stared directly into the lens, not blinking. He picked at the beer can with his thumbnail, as though it possessed a paper label. "Betty ain't a large woman, you know, but down on the floor, blocking the door, all tucked into a ball, she was what you might call concentrated weight. Dead weight. I could see enough through the window, what with the sun and all being that low in the sky. Hand to God, I seen something I never seen before and hope I don't live to see again. The woman's thumb was smoking. Little puffs coming off it. Looking like the butt end of an old cigar. I was in the army, in combat, and I never saw a thing like that. So I leaned hard on the door and shoved her over enough to let myself inside. Betty wasn't breathing. Her chest wasn't going up and down under her shirt. She was all covered with mud. I knew she was dead. Nobody had to tell me—I just knew. That is something I don't wish on any man, seeing his wife muddy and dead. But—and this is how you know I was still thinking clear—her thumb was putting off smoke, like I said, and the smoke smelled like shit. That's how I knew she hadn't been gone long, what with that smoke curling off the end of her black thumb. Whatever had happened to Betty happened just a little bit ago. I knew that from the smoking thumb." Fred held his own out-of-focus thumb toward the camera lens.

"I figured I had to go with the mouth-to-mouth. And you know how I wear one of those surgery mask things when I cut the grass? Too much dust and grass in the air. My lungs close up, and if I don't get an inhaler quick enough, hell, I'll be the one dead on the ground. Betty was turning whiter while I stood there looking at her, so I leaned down and pushed my mask up on my forehead. Then," Fred paused. "Then, I started thinking about it." He jerked his head toward the kitchen. "Maybe you ought to get the beer this time."

Gable stopped the camera, checked the timer, and realized that he was about to fill the memory card. He wondered if Fred had an ending nearby. He thought he should probably give Fred something to eat, so he grabbed a bag of chips from the pantry, ripped open the top, and dumped them in a bowl. Gable moved fast between rooms.

"Those aren't salt and vinegar, are they? Salt and vinegar chips give me gas, but I do love 'em," Fred said when Gable returned. Without waiting for an answer, Fred tried to restart the story before Gable had the camera running.

Gable held his hand up. "Calm down. Have some chips. They're regular. I'm almost ready," Gable said, settling into his chair and adjusting his headphones. He pointed at Fred. "Okay, you mentioned mouth-to-mouth."

"I do like this couch, Gable. Kind of molds around your backside. It wasn't the idea of doing mouth-to-mouth that got to me, you see. Think about being with somebody over fifty years. I probably had my mouth on every inch of that woman at some point in time, but we're both staring down eighty. Listen to me. You're kneeling there, your knees aching and you're looking down at your wife and her thumb's putting off smoke and there's that damn burnt skin smell. You begin to think for a minute. You can't help but think. You think about how she ain't never happy with the way the yard looks and how she tells you to drive faster to church even though you probably shouldn't be driving at all and how she don't even worry about her hair anymore, just keeps coloring it red and letting it bunch up on top like some kind of circus clown. You think about how the two of you have lived together so long, you never thought there was any other way to live. So, I waited a minute, didn't do nothing. Then, you start thinking, who'll fix my supper and who'll get out of bed to turn up the heat in the middle of the night and who'll start my bath in the evenings?" Fred stuck a fistful of chips in his mouth. The crunching sounded like thunder in Gable's headphones.

"I leaned down and laid my head right on Betty's chest. It was quiet under her shirt. Maybe, just maybe, I heard a little air moving around in there. I couldn't tell. Might've imagined it. I was breathing pretty hard myself. Maybe Betty was dead and gone, maybe not. I sat there thinking, still deciding what to do. I thought about crying."

Gable pushed in tighter on Fred's face. "You cried?"

"I said I *thought* about it. I used to know how many presses on the chest I'm supposed to do after I blow a couple of breaths into her mouth. I read that in some magazine one time or another. I'm sitting there and I caught me a whiff of that thumb, which had thankfully stopped smoking, but the stink of it was enough to gag me. You ever smell burnt skin?" Before Gable had time to say he hadn't, Fred continued. "I could hire somebody, I thought. Plenty of people looking for jobs taking care of somebody like me."

"Betty?" Gable said.

"Oh, well, the lipstick on Betty's mouth was all cracked and smeared. There wasn't any color left in her face, only in her ears, so red they almost glowed. The burnt thumb smell climbed up in the back of my throat. I couldn't wait any more, couldn't think about it anymore. So, I put my hand over her mouth and her nose at the same time. Just to be sure. I still wasn't positive about what I heard inside her chest, whether it was air or not. So I did what I did. I put as much of her face as I could under my palm and pressed down and looked the other way and waited for time to pass."

Gable wasn't sure he'd heard right. "Come again?"

Fred appeared flustered for a second. His hand twirled in front of him before he started talking. "Maybe I ought not to have told you that. At the time, it seemed like the thing to do, so dammit that's what I did. I waited for maybe half a minute. Just waited with my hand over her mouth and her nose. Turns out, covering up her entire face probably brought her back. I covered up that lipstick and that nose of hers and all the sudden, Betty starts hacking and spitting behind my hand, trying to suck air into her mouth. I jerk away, and she opens her eyes, big and mostly white, like a baby looking up from a crib. And now, she can't thank me enough for saving her life. How's that for love, neighbor?" Fred turned the can up again. "No harm, no foul, and sometimes you come out smelling like a goddamn rose, even if you tried to smother your own wife."

Gable stared at Fred through the viewfinder, waiting for him to say he'd been kidding, that he'd really given his breath to Betty and reined her back from the dead. But Fred didn't move. Gable noticed a quiet alarm coming from the camera, signaling the end of the memory. How long the warning had been sounding was anybody's guess.

?

From the edge of his yard, Gable watched Fred head home, leaning heavily on the walker to keep his balance. He waved at him even though Fred wasn't looking. Gable decided he needed a walk around the block. He wandered through the round pools of light from the streetlights, thinking about Fred's story. He thought about suffocation.

In those first days after Hollis left, Gable felt as though he couldn't breathe, like he couldn't possibly bring enough air into his chest to survive another day. Then, when he found out about the man she'd been seeing for months and months before the separation, the weight evaporated instantly, magically. He suddenly had a reason everything went wrong. Bad news brought him back to life, and he could gulp in air once more.

Fred made him realize this. For half a minute, Fred had tried to kill Betty and, in the process, reeled her back to life. Had Hollis done the same thing for him? *No*, Gable thought, *it's completely different. It has something to do with love, but it's completely different*. Gable wondered what Betty felt, lying on her floor, her eyes shut, hoping she'd remember how to breathe again.

Gable found himself in front of Laurie's house, at the edge of the shadows on the street. He saw glimpses of kids flashing behind the window shades and thought he heard Laurie yelling at them to slow down. He didn't know the story of Laurie's marriage. That subject hadn't come up. Gable assumed that one person, at some point, had made it difficult for the other to breathe.

He stood in the street, studying her windows, wondering if she was suffocating in a house where children sprinted up and down the hallway until bedtime. Gable was still confused, but he suddenly knew sometimes it wasn't about love anymore. It was about breathing out and breathing in.

❖

The only thing he missed on-camera, it turned out, was Fred's final gulp of beer and a dramatic crushing of the can. Gable stayed up late the next night, batching the clips of Fred into a single folder and downloading them into his editing program. He watched Fred tell the story over and over. Gable was surprised at what he'd forgotten, how Fred's eyes darted to the far corner of the room as he talked about sealing off his wife's airway, how he'd racked the focus once on Fred's hands during the story, at one of the rare moments when they weren't winging around.

Fred didn't return for a couple of days, didn't shuffle across the street in the afternoons, but Gable wasn't worried. He saw Fred in his yard, slowly ferrying a bag of garbage to the dumpster or doing laps on his riding lawn mower.

Then, one afternoon, Betty returned in a quiet ambulance. Gable didn't see any of the neighbors watching. They must have known this was a drop-off, not a pick-up. Much less exciting. Fred leaned on his walker in the driveway, directing the two men who pushed Betty's gurney toward the side entrance. Fred waved across the street at Gable and motioned him over.

"Come say how do," Fred called out as Gable crossed the street. "Betty's back. She's going to tell you everything about her thumb. You won't even have to ask." He rolled his eyes behind his glasses.

Inside, the two ambulance company employees settled Betty on her bed, then left Gable and Fred standing beside her. Fred patted her on the shoulder. "The new hip's coming along and the ribs only hurt when she laughs, so she's pretty much pain-free there," he said. "She's never been much of a laugher."

"Fred tells me you been making a star out of him," Betty said to Gable, her voice thin and brittle, without the normal volume.

"Oh, yeah, I'm trying," Gable answered, laughing and noticing that he didn't sound like himself. The camera ran in the palm of his hand. He knew he had the angle right to catch Betty in the frame. He only hoped there was enough light in the room.

"I can tell you what it's like to be dead and brought back. You should get that on your camera. Fred brought me back, you know. He probably didn't tell you about that. He doesn't like talking about what happened. He's too modest, but I remember it all," Betty said, tapping her temple with her finger. "Oh, you should get this thumb in your movie. Doctor says it will never be the same again. I'll be scarred for life."

Fred sat beside her on the bed. Without glancing down, Gable widened the angle so he could frame both of them in the picture. The sun shifted slightly behind the blinds, dipping into the limbs outside her window. Fred appeared happy to have her back in the house, back in their bedroom. He couldn't stop touching her arm or stroking her shoulder. Gable thought about Fred's story. He wondered how long they could live together without both of them knowing what really happened in the basement.

"Just wasn't your time, dearie," Fred said. "We all punch a different time clock."

"When I'm settled in, you come on over and I'll tell you all about it," Betty said, "and you can put it in your movie. A week or so maybe. Right now, I need to do my thumb exercises. I saw your yard when I pulled in, neighbor. You got it looking good." Betty stuck her bandaged thumb right in Gable's face and wiggled the gauze for him.

That night, Gable sat in front of the computer, scanning and downloading. He trashed video clips of downspouts and mosquitoes to free up memory for footage about love. More than once, he butted clips together in various combinations, rejected their order, and started over.

In the quiet, he heard the noises his house made—the metallic tick of the air conditioner as it cycled off, the roof joists creaking as the night grew cooler, the floorboards shifting in the hallway. Once, the cicadas became so loud outside that Gable walked to the window to see if he could spot any of them landing on the tree trunks to lose their skins. He noticed lights at the Randalls'. It was long after midnight. Gable imagined it must be difficult to sleep with broken ribs. Maybe Fred was waking up now and then to make sure his wife was still breathing next to him.

Gable shuffled the video clips, hoping a perfect combination would suddenly fall together. Finally, he decided on a plan. He would make a series of scenes. He would take random clips from Fred, from Laurie, and from Betty, then place them one right after the other, in that same order, again and again, without previewing them. Fred, Laurie, Betty. Fred, Laurie, Betty. Just to see.

> *Fred says he moved Betty away from the door.*
> *Laurie walks across the front of the camera, naked, and returns in a couple of seconds with the vodka bottle and sits down on the couch, smiling.*
> *Betty says Gable is making a star out of Fred.*
>
> *Fred says he put his hand over Betty's mouth.*
> *Laurie closes her eyes and touches the scar on her belly and recites the exact time of birth for each of her children.*
> *Betty says she has to do her thumb exercises.*
>
> *Fred says it wasn't your time, dearie.*

Laurie gathers up her clothes and says she has to let the sitter go and that she's getting up early tomorrow anyway. She says she likes to run before the children are awake.

Betty opens her eyes to the camera as the EMS people roll her to the ambulance.

Fred says it was quiet under Betty's shirt, but maybe, just maybe....

Laurie smiles and tells the camera not to expect her to get naked every time they get together then stretches and slips her sports bra over her shoulders.

Betty says she can tell you what it is like to be dead and brought back to life.

And that was it. A running time just shy of four minutes. Gable watched it a couple of times before he output the digital video to a CD. Once it burned, he labeled it with a Sharpie: *Gable's Love Movie*. He didn't have any spare jewel cases, so he found a music CD he never listened to and threw the cover art and the lyric sheets in the trash.

He drove to Hollis's duplex and spent several minutes deciding if he really wanted to leave the CD for his ex-wife. It was almost five in the morning. He sat in the shadows on her curb. He knew his little movie said something important to Hollis, but he was sure she wouldn't get it. She wouldn't recognize love. She wouldn't understand the suffocation. Gable wasn't even sure *he* understood his footage, didn't know if the CD meant he was over Hollis or just beginning to realize he never would be. At least he could breathe better now. A breeze suddenly sprang up, chattering the leaves in the pin oaks and poplars that canopied the street.

Okay, Gable thought, *maybe it's all those things. You cover a mouth, yet someone survives. Babies leave a scar on you as they enter the world. You throw a switch, and your thumb burns forever. The person you least want to leave says she has to go and the best you can do is watch her go down the driveway.*

Gable climbed back in his car and drove toward home. He slowed at the curb in front of the Randalls' house. For a second, he thought of sailing the CD into their yard like the morning paper, leaving it for Fred to find after dawn. *Let him figure out what to do with it,* Gable thought. Instead, he continued to roll quietly, winding through the streets toward Laurie's house, thinking he would leave it in her mailbox. Let her see what the local Spielberg turned out. Maybe one night they could watch it together on the plaid couch. But he never so much as tapped the brake.

When he found himself reaching for the blinker yet again, he realized he was driving odd circles around and around his own neighborhood, *Gable's Love Movie* still sitting on the seat next to him, still waiting for someone to watch it.

III

Oxygen

Morgan kept a running list on his refrigerator.

The current title of the list was: *Most Distressing Things That Have Happened To Me*—current because *distressing* was the sixth different word he had used. Crossed out with a pencil were the others he'd rejected through the years: embarrassing, infuriating, confounding, confusing, and traumatizing. The list contained incidents you would probably expect from less than half a lifetime, like the unfortunate urination misunderstanding in the sixth-grade cafeteria or the time he walked in on his parents having sex (not in their bedroom, but in the oily-smelling garage, splayed across the hood of the Country Squire station wagon like unlucky deer) or his lurking erectile dysfunction, which, by the way, he blamed squarely on the Country Squire episode. But this? This man—the man in Morgan's basement apartment, unconscious and still attached to the colon-cleaning machine—might cause him to flip through his dog-eared *Roget's Thesaurus* and come up with a whole new vocabulary.

Like the colon-cleaning machine, the basement apartment was part of Morgan's new beginning. The idea of living below someone appealed to him, so he rented the apartment sight unseen after reading a small ad in the local newspaper. He talked to a man on the phone, the man who now lived above him. On the phone, his prospective landlord, a Mr. Sutton, sounded as though he was in a hurry to be somewhere else, gasping out his sentences rather than speaking them. He asked if there was anything in particular he should know about Morgan's past that would keep him from renting the apartment. Morgan briefly thought about his obsession with his refrigerator list but decided against going into personal details. (He was unsure about confidentiality and renter's rights and the like.) Mr. Sutton sucked in some air and quickly asked if Morgan was on any sexual offenders list. Morgan laughed, again thinking about his list, specifically number seven, the erectile dysfunction, and the impractical irony of being a sexual predator with consistently flagging motivation. Mr. Sutton took the laugh for a no, and Morgan moved in the following weekend.

Now, Morgan spent hours lying on his mattress, staring at the exposed floor joists and charting Mr. Sutton's life. Immediately after moving in, he realized how mistaken he was from the phone conversation; Mr. Sutton *never* went anywhere in a hurry. He heard him shuffling from room to room, tugging his oxygen tank behind him. He heard him turn on the television and try to make it to the bathroom during the commercials. He heard him telephone his children. He heard him talking to his dead wife at night as he snuck a cigarette on the small deck just off his kitchen. Mr. Sutton never really spoke with Morgan, simply removed the check Morgan taped to his door on the first of every month.

This was the only type of voyeur Morgan could ever be, one who lay very still and imagined most of the scenes. Of course, the short wanderings of Mr. Sutton's life weren't the only sounds Morgan was forced to deal with. The pipes that ran along the basement ceiling clanked and pinged at all times of the day. The house above him settled every now and again, cracking thinly on its foundations, especially when there was a change in the weather. Sometimes, Morgan imagined he heard fresh mildew growing down the far wall, which held back the small hill outside and tended to catch all the rain runoff. He complained to Mr. Sutton about the mildew once. Mr. Sutton told Morgan to move somewhere above ground if he didn't want underground problems.

But this unconscious man on the table was a problem that Morgan had not foreseen. Of course, foresight had never been a core competency of Morgan's. If he'd possessed this quality, the list on his refrigerator would be much shorter. He would have realized that installing a colon-cleaning machine in his basement was not a wise career move, but he was, in a word, desperate. His money, the few thousand dollars that remained from his father's life insurance payout, was running dangerously low. Renting the apartment *and* purchasing the El Camino had drained his bank account considerably. He couldn't resist the El Camino, though. It called to him like a metallic Siren from the used car lot on Washington Street.

Morgan had always believed the El Camino was the most practical American car ever built, more than likely the brainchild of a bipolar automobile designer who simply couldn't make up his mind and concocted a bastardized hybrid: half sedan, half pickup truck. Morgan had lusted after El Caminos for years, and, suddenly, with money in his pocket and longing in his heart, he found one he could afford. It possessed minimal rust, a decent-sounding transmission, and the paint—that semi-gold that Chevrolet experimented with in the 70s—was only slightly faded. Morgan thought the car fit him perfectly.

The only hitch in the transaction turned out to be the girl behind the counter. The salesman, Artie the Used Car King, told Morgan that "my gal inside will handle all the paperwork." Morgan expected a sleepy-eyed, desk-anchored woman who had given up on satisfying employment and settled for a little floor space inside a mobile home on a car lot. Morgan never saw it coming. What he found inside was the poster child for annoying energy. The girl—definitely not a woman or a *gal*—never stood still, bouncing from desktop to door to chair like a pinball ricocheting off the flipper. When she stopped moving for a second, Morgan saw a stick-on name tag that read *Hi. My name is Cici*. He wondered if she made herself a new name tag every morning. She shook her dreadlocks at him.

"I'm Cici," she jabbered, pointing at her nametag. "You get a deal? Hope so. Every once in a while, you can get a deal from the King. We gotta fill out some papers. Get you a temporary tag. You financing? Paying cash? Wow, you're tall. I'm Cici." She ran toward Morgan, her hand pointed ahead of her like a lance. *She is so thin, she must be brittle*, Morgan thought as he shook lightly and took a seat. He had never purchased a car before, always content with hand-me-down autos from his parents. (The only time he ever refused their generosity was when they offered him the massive Country Squire.)

Cici grabbed a few sheets of paper and shoved them in front of him during one of her fly-bys. "What'd you buy? What number?" She scratched her scalp with the end of a pen, then handed it to Morgan.

"Thirty-seven," he answered, smiling at the thought of his new car. Cici came to a stop as if she'd been shot with a tranquilizer dart.

"Shit," she said. "Not thirty-seven. Not the El Cee! Please..."

"Well, yeah. The El Camino."

"Man, this is a complication of massive import." She actually sat down and let out a heavy sigh. Morgan noticed that silver studs decorated the edge of one of her ears.

"It was for sale, right? I mean, I didn't mean to do anything—"

"Nah, man. It's just that, you know, you try to make a plan, and the cosmos plots against you, you know what I mean? The planets don't align." The studs didn't stop at her ear. As she talked, Morgan noticed the thick one in the center of her tongue. "I was going to use the El Cee to move some stuff. Artie lets me use a car sometimes."

Morgan sensed a surprising flutter in his crotch, so surprising that he actually glanced down at his jeans. Maybe he could actually do something nice for this girl, and after that, who knew?

"Well, hey, I could help you out. With stuff or whatever. No need to worry about that." He tried to look matter-of-fact. Cici smiled at him and jumped to her feet.

"That is so cool," she said. "See? Cosmos and karma. Sometimes they work out. You never know. Thanks, man." She smiled again as she began pacing laps around the tiny room. Morgan's flutter evolved into out-and-out hydraulics for a happy few seconds, and Morgan thought that he could never be this fortunate: new apartment, an El Camino, and a silver-tongued girl with too much energy (too much even for the hood of a Country Squire), all in the space of one week?

?

The day of the accident with the colon-cleaning machine, he called Cici at the CopyShop. She'd quit Artie's weeks ago and took a job behind the counter so she could sneak free flyers in a variety of colors, advertising the colon-cleaning machine business. She even used pilfered CopyShop staples to tack the flyers on telephone poles around town. Before Morgan could say anything important, she reminded him about making personal calls to the CopyShop and how one girl was actually fired for the offense.

"But you don't understand. This may be an emergency," he said. "I think I may have come close to killing this guy with the machine." In the few seconds of silence, a chorus of copy machines hummed low in the background. Morgan decided to keep talking. "He's out cold. The hoses are still hooked up."

"Man," Cici said.

Morgan wanted to say it was her fault, that she should have never let him practice colonic therapy on his own this soon. (He would have to admit that he was genuinely interested in the whole process.) To be honest, it was not Cici's fault. The root of Morgan's enthusiasm landed squarely on the shoulders of Norman W. Walker, D.Sc., Ph.D. and his book, *Colon Health: The Key to a Vibrant Life*. Cici loaned Morgan her signed copy of the book the night he helped her store the colon machine in his basement. That was why she'd needed the El Camino, to move the two large boxes of hoses and gauges and one medium backpack out of her girlfriend's house. "The machine is the last meaningful thing that connects us, so to speak. I'm really trying to break free."

Morgan took the revelation that Cici was an energetic lesbian rather well. No romantic devastation. The fact that he had experienced a positive reaction to a woman's presence (lesbian or not) was encouragement enough. He and Cici had become quick friends and business partners not two blocks from the girlfriend's house.

"This is so cool, Morgan," she said that first afternoon, bouncing in the seat. "You've got water hookups right there in the basement. Hot and cold. A drain in the floor. I can get some fabric. Make a little dressing room and a cleaning room. We'll need a table and some sheets. It was easy at Lucy's. She had all that stuff. But we can get it for ourselves, right? Can we unload it right now? I'm so psyched to get started, man. I'm certified in colonics, you know? You probably already guessed that." Morgan surmised that people who undergo colon-cleaning must enjoy constant chatter from the machine operator. Cici never shut up.

Morgan did manage to slip in that they couldn't possibly unload the boxes until Mr. Sutton either went down for his nap or out for his weekly respiratory therapy appointment, which would take place the next day. He didn't want to raise any red flags with his landlord. They decided to store the boxes in the El Camino overnight and use the next afternoon to set up the equipment. Cici refused to let Morgan drive her home, preferring to walk.

"But how far is it?" he asked.

"Well, I'm not really sure. It's my new place. I've never been from here to there. Listen, I walk everywhere. It's how I stay in touch with the earth." She pushed her tongue stud against her lower teeth, and it popped out toward Morgan like a silver exclamation point. Then, she shouldered her backpack and turned down the sidewalk.

Morgan read Walker's book from cover to cover, beginning with the author's opening poem, "The Story of The Solon Concerning His Colon," and ending with the final chapter, "The Ghastly Result of Neglecting the Colon." As he lay there, his reading interrupted only by Mr. Sutton and his oxygen tank making their way to the kitchen for some sort of snack (Morgan heard the refrigerator door slam shut), Morgan considered his chance meeting with Cici and his momentary erectile function and even let his mind wander to his ex-wife and the way her hair turned the most wonderful streaks of colors in the summer. He considered putting down the book and turning his attention to himself when Chapter 8 conveniently exposed itself: "The Reproductive Organs and their Effect on the Colon." Under the subsection "Male Organs: The Testes," Morgan saw this passage:

> When one considers that the period of reproducing a single orgasm or discharge of the semen requires an average of 35 days, it can readily be appreciated why the excessive discharge of this semen causes weakness, and

> when deliberately exercised by an adult may cause premature loss of the ability to function sexually. All too often weakness and senility is the result of a lifelong abuse of such a practice. (p. 91)

And further down the page:

> Man's virility depends upon his conservation of the sperm, not his ability to waste it. Marriage laws and the commandment against adultery were promulgated with this end in view. (p. 91)

Morgan decided it was best to simply go to sleep, and the next morning he and Cici discreetly moved her boxes into his basement apartment. She arranged the hoses and gauges to her liking and, just like that, they were in business. Smoothly.

Until this morning.

"I need more of a response than 'man,' Cici," he said to her. He heard a CopyShop customer ask for the location of the bathroom. Cici must have pointed because Morgan didn't hear her respond. She came back on the phone.

"Did you use the Foot Relaxation Chart?"

"Yes, yes. I did exactly what you showed me. Cici, this is bad. Has this ever happened to you?" Morgan glanced at the man face down on the table. His chest rose and fell, but just barely. His ponytail dangled awkwardly across one shoulder.

"How long has he been out?" she wanted to know.

"Just a couple of minutes. I called you right away. I can't really call an ambulance, you know?" Morgan wanted to stay calm, but he was sweating, even in the clammy chill of the basement. He went over the process in his head, the checklist of colonics. He had monitored the water temperature constantly. His fluid application had been deliberate, a bit over a pint at a time. He was only three to three-and-a-half gallons into the procedure. He applied steady pressure to the proper location on the bottom of the foot to facilitate nerve relaxation and release in the colon area. He remembered hearing Mr. Sutton ambling toward the bathroom during the foot massage, remembered hearing the double flush.

"Oh my god," Morgan whispered into the phone.

"He didn't just die, did he?"

"No. Oh my god, Sutton flushed," Morgan felt himself going pale. "Upstairs. While our water was running."

"Man, no telling what that does to the temperature and the pressure," Cici said. "That's never happened with me, you know. We didn't think of that. Details. Shit. Are you, like, freaking out?"

Morgan sensed that Cici was trying to distance herself from the man on the table. "What would *you* be doing, huh? In fact, that's a good question. What would you do? You need to get down here."

"I don't go on break until eleven. Things happen for a reason, you know. Uh oh, here comes Max. I got to go," and Cici hung up on Morgan.

First things first, Morgan thought. *First, take the hose and the adapter out of the man's ass.* So he did. And the man didn't flinch or make a sound. And he was still breathing. Morgan had sometimes wondered what people meant when they described someone's breathing as *shallow*. This, he realized, is most definitely shallow, tiny puffs of air that seem to come not from the lungs, but from some place far away. Morgan heard Mr. Sutton pulling his oxygen tank trailer across the hardwood floors.

Oxygen! Morgan thought.

The next moments were a blur. Morgan backed the El Camino as close as possible to the door of the basement apartment. Lucky for him, it was relatively early on a Saturday morning, not many people out in their yards, not many people who could possibly see Morgan slide his twin mattress into the bed of the El Camino, then deadlift a man on top of it. *He's skinny. That's fortunate, I suppose,* Morgan thought. He laid the man on his back and watched him smiling in the direction of the sky. He wondered what the man could possibly be dreaming about that would make him smile. His color looked better.

Morgan decided he had a couple of options. He could drop the man off at the CopyShop, make a big scene and embarrass/infuriate/confound/confuse/traumatize Cici, who started all of this. Or, he could drop the man off at the emergency room, which would be risky; he couldn't take a chance that he'd eventually be confronted by a policeman at the ER.

If his parole officer caught wind of something like this, Morgan would be sent back to jail tomorrow, which would please his ex-wife. She'd never thought he received enough of a sentence. So many times, Morgan tried to describe to her that feeling, the one he experienced when he walked in on her and the boyfriend. Sure, sure, Morgan and his wife were already legally divorced, but he still had a key, and that particular evening, he had a head full of middle-drawer vodka, but he never expected to find his ex-wife squirming beneath the boyfriend. At least it wasn't a smelly garage and the hood of a Country Squire, but the difference this time was that he could do something other than close the door and slink away to his room. He could teach somebody a lesson about boundaries and crossing them, even if he was the one making up the boundaries. It was the only time he'd ever gotten that physical. The incident became number nine on the current refrigerator list: "Getting 90 Days for Assaulting the Boyfriend."

So, unless he anonymously dumped the guy at the door like a FedEx package, the emergency room was not an option.

Morgan covered the man in the bed of his El Camino with a blanket, tucked it under his chin, and glanced up in time to see Mr. Sutton staring from his side window. His eyes were large. Morgan waved at him and motioned him to the door.

Mr. Sutton peered through his peephole. Morgan called out. "Can I borrow your tank for a second?"

"Who is that naked hippie in your truck?" Sutton asked.

Morgan hated it when people called the El Camino a truck. Under normal circumstances, he would explain the differences. "A friend. I think he fainted."

Sutton didn't move from the peephole, wanting to keep an eye on Morgan. "Right. A friend. Were you and that girl doing that butt thing on him?"

Morgan felt suddenly weak in the knees. Sutton knew all along what they were up to in the basement. "No," he said. "I mean, how did you find out about that?"

The door opened. Sutton stood there bent over like a doll, plastic nose clips feeding him oxygen. His eyes were puffy and bloodshot. Morgan wondered if it was due to lack of air. Or too much air. "Are you fucking kidding me? I hear everything through the vents. You talk to yourself way too freaking much, by the way."

And I believed I was the only voyeur, Morgan thought. "Okay, yes, I was doing a colonic treatment on this guy, and he must have fainted. I think it happened when you flushed the commode."

Sutton interrupted. "I wondered if that would affect your pressure. I used to be a civil engineer, you know."

"I need to get him some help. I thought oxygen would be a good thing. Maybe you could drive us to the hospital. I'll ride with you. No, I'll even ride in the back with the guy. You could really help me out, Mr. Sutton."

Mr. Sutton reached forward and pushed Morgan aside slightly, so he could see down the side of his house.

"You don't need my help," he said, taking a halting half-breath. "Look there. You don't have a problem anymore."

Morgan turned in the direction Mr. Sutton pointed. The man in the back of Morgan's El Camino was no longer breathing shallow. In fact, he was no longer in the back of Morgan's El Camino. He was running down the street, trailing Morgan's blanket behind him like a makeshift Superman cape, carrying his belongings in a bundle in his arms. He must have ducked back inside to grab his things. But he didn't take time to put on his pants, which Morgan found odd.

"Your car is still idling," Mr. Sutton said. Morgan knew he should do something. This was a moment that called for action. Morgan's first instinct was to chase after the man, not so much to catch him, but rather, to ask him where he went during his brief, colon-induced vacation and why he was smiling so broadly during his unconscious time away. *But*, Morgan thought, *he has too much of a head start.* This was the first time Morgan noticed his patient had arrived on foot that morning, that he had not parked in the driveway or on the street.

"He moves pretty good for a skinny guy," Mr. Sutton added, closing the door.

?

Morgan retreated to his mildewy apartment and sat on the edge of his bed frame. When he was in jail, he was required to receive counseling once a week for anger management, even though he tried to explain that the only time he was truly mad in his entire life was the moment he saw his ex-wife and the boyfriend. His counselor was a man named Stovitch. He had an Iron Curtain stare and shoulders that smacked of weight training. Morgan liked him.

The one thing that Stovitch told him, the one thing that continued to blare inside his head, was his theory of accounting. He said that Morgan should, on a regular basis, sit calmly and take stock of what he possessed at that particular moment. He said that by listing physical, material, and emotional assets, "you can balance the books inside your head and your soul and thus create a more harmonious life. It's balance and equilibrium, but you can't have balance and equilibrium if you don't take an accounting every once in a while, hmmm?" Stovitch *hmmm*ed at the end of his longer sentences for effect.

While Morgan always respected his advice, he had never put it into practice until today, after watching the skinny, pony-tailed Superman sprinting down the sidewalk. Morgan sat and did some accounting.

He had a criminal record. He had an ex-wife. He had the makings of a colonic clinic in his basement apartment. (Which meant he had a basement apartment.) He had a landlord who was running short of air. He had a business partner who was an adrenaline-junkie lesbian. He had an anemic bank account and little hope of resurrecting it. He had a used El Camino. That was about it. No job. No friends. Way too much time to himself. Oh, and he had a copy of Walker's book on the bed beside him, which he flipped through. A paragraph in Chapter 3, "Colon Therapy," caught his eye:

> Do not expect one or two colon irrigations to revitalize your system if you have neglected to take care of its excreta for 20, 30, or even 60 or 80 years, any more than you would expect a pill to cause all your ailments and troubles to vanish overnight. (p. 12)

Walker's words slammed into Morgan like a hammerhead. Walker was speaking to him, right from the pages of *The Key to a Vibrant Life*. There *was* too much excreta in Morgan's life, too much to fix according to Stovitch's simple accounting principles. He had nothing at stake, nothing up for grabs in his little world. Any normal person would probably kill themselves. Morgan decided that Dr. Walker had already condemned him to an early grave due to excessive excreta and, at that precise moment, at that colonic epiphany, he spied his client's wallet beneath the edge of the colon-cleaning table, no doubt the place it fell when he grabbed his pants and fled. That, Morgan concluded, was an omen that could not be ignored.

It took him only seconds to remove the mattress from the bed of the El Camino. Mr. Sutton watched from the upper window. Ironically, the address on the driver's license was mere blocks away—well within naked-running distance—but Morgan felt the need to be surrounded by metal, by the gentle groan of the El Camino.

He had never glanced at the colonic patient information sheet previously or Morgan would have known that his fainter was named Owen Morris of 737 Turnbuckle Court. Morgan even had a good idea of which house belonged to Mr. Morris: the Tudor with the crumbling stucco sat at the far end of the cul-de-sac, almost daring traffic to come toward its dead end.

Morgan parked and walked to the front door. With a quick, nonchalant glance through the big window (so as not to attract the attention of crime patrol neighbors), he saw a living room that appeared rarely used and, beyond that, a breakfast nook near what must have been a kitchen. The interior seemed bright and cheery and not the tone that one would associate with a man who wore a ponytail and snuck out on Saturday morning to have his colon flushed.

Morgan rang the bell and heard quick steps approach the door. A young girl peered around the crack she made. "Mommy, it's a man!" she yelled.

"I'm here to see your daddy," Morgan said, remembering to smile. "I found his wallet."

"Mommy, it's someone for Daddy!" she yelled again. "My name is Amanda. He's coming I think." Amanda shut the door and, just as quickly, it reopened. Owen Morris stood framed in the doorway. He was not expecting to see Morgan. "Oh," was all he said. His eyes began to vibrate with panic.

"I found your wallet, Mr. Morris. I thought you would probably want it before you had to start calling all the credit card companies and whatever," Morgan said very officially.

"Oh. Oh my," Owen answered. He reached out and took the wallet Morgan held forward like a handshake. Owen opened his wallet and fumbled with some bills. He lowered his voice to a whisper. "I realized too late that I had, well, left without paying you for anything. I don't know what happened. I'm so embarrassed."

"We think it was the water pressure. And maybe the temperature. You don't owe me anything. I'm just glad you are alright. Nothing to be embarrassed about," Morgan said, suddenly feeling better about doing a good thing. From the back of the house, a voice called for Owen.

"Nothing, dear. Someone found my wallet," he yelled over his shoulder.

As Morgan turned to leave, Amanda peeked around the door again, her eyes big against the wood. Morgan realized one of the things his life was missing. Not a daughter, per se, but someone to answer his door, someone to watch the gate, so to speak.

On the ride back to his apartment, Morgan thought clearly, which he found odd. In the short distance, he formulated a plan that seemed to make sense as he drove along the blocks. It took him only half an hour to disassemble the machine and repack it into its original boxes. He loaded these in the El Camino. Another hour, and his clothes and all the belongings he truly cared about were inside a duffel bag and tucked behind the bench seat. He knew the awkward part would be telling Mr. Sutton he was breaking his lease. He hadn't heard the oxygen tank scraping its way along his ceiling, but Morgan wasn't worried. Mr. Sutton often napped at odd times.

Morgan checked the apartment one last time, making sure anything left behind remained on purpose. During this final walk-through, he heard Sutton above him, out on the small deck, conversing with his dead wife. Morgan slid a chair to the ceiling nearest the deck and stood as close as he could to the sound. Mr. Sutton asked his dead wife how she was feeling, if her sore back was better, if she had begun to sleep through the night yet. (He said he remembered how she was with strange surroundings and her sleep rhythms.) Then, Morgan heard his landlord tell his wife about the events of the morning, how he was asked to be of help, but then the man in trouble sprinted down the street, his bare backside to the world. Mr. Sutton laughed and lost his breath and waited for a response from heaven. "I know, I know. I wish you had been here to see it, too," he offered up.

Morgan ripped out the opening page of Dr. Walker's book and circled the first paragraph with a pen:

> Your body is the house in which you live. By analogy, it is just like the building in which you make your home. Your home needs, at the very least, periodical attention, other-

> wise the roof may leak, the plumbing may get out of order and clog up, termites will drill through the floors and the walls, and other innumerable cases of deterioration will make their appearance. Such is the case with your physical body. Every function and activity of your system, day and night, physical, mental, and spiritual, is dependent on the attention you give to it. (p. 1)

He walked quietly up the small slope and taped the page to Mr. Sutton's door. He could hear him inside, still talking with his wife. The faint odor of cigarette smoke slid beneath the threshold.

He made the call to Cici's new apartment. She'd only paid the first month's rent. There wasn't even a cleaning deposit required. Morgan thought he would have to talk her into the whole thing, but, in retrospect, he realized that Cici had a knack for surprising people.

She waited for him at the sidewalk, her backpack looped around her shoulder. In her free arm, she cradled a dog, a distinctive mix of Chihuahua and dachshund with maybe a hint of terrier. Morgan rolled to a slow stop and threw open the passenger door. Cici stuck her head in. "You know I'm a lesbian, right?"

"Yes," he said, "but I didn't know you had a dog."

She glanced at the creature in the crook of her arm. "He's new. I found him twenty minutes after I was fired from the CopyShop. Did I mention I got fired?

Anyway, we were meant to be. It's a sign. I decided to call him Toner." She climbed in and laid Toner on the seat between them. The dog growled at Morgan, circled himself twice, and settled into his newest space.

"Did you ever see this?" Morgan handed Cici his list of *Most Distressing Things That Have Happened To Me*. She began to read as he wound his way from the parking lot to the highway. The windows were down, and the air was beginning to blow through the cab. He was up to a good cruising speed on the edge of town when she balled up the page and tossed it through the open window of the El Camino. "Fuck that," she said.

"I just remembered," Morgan said, smiling and looking in the rear-view mirror to see where the list landed. "I'm breaking my parole."

"Whatever," Cici said, petting Toner again and again on his bony haunch. "Stuff has a way of working out."

Morgan knew beyond a shadow of a doubt, at that particular moment, he was the only minor fugitive in the world on the road with a lesbian and a mutt beside him and a colon-cleaning machine strapped into the bed of an El Camino. He drew a deep full breath of the air rushing by him. He felt wanted and reckless and needed for the first time in a long, long time, and it made him drive even faster—faster than he probably should, considering.

The Prince

I will now proceed with appropriate background because I have discovered in previous retellings of this tale, a lack of background results in confusion, especially at the point of the second jumper cable incident. And while in most cases I despise peering backward (an act that accomplishes nothing, it seems, except wasting time), I do feel that background clears up many potentially lingering questions.

Brian agrees and will adopt a holding pattern in the rocker beside me as I explain the reasons we are here. He will also be in charge of pouring whilst I speak.

The background starts here: Some eleven months ago, during the weighty heat of early August, my wife took leave of her senses and our house.

(Brian will no doubt interject at this point that in this part of the country, it is never the heat, it's always the humidity that gets you.)

Gathering some personal belongings and minimal warm-weather provisions, most of them hastily packed into a minivan with a manual transmission she couldn't decipher, my dearly beloved ground metal down the driveway after more than a decade and a half of marriage, during which we suffered the requisite emotional ups and downs of cohabitation resulting from lack of money or an overabundance of bad fortune or fear of an uncertain and penurious future.

Two lovely children resulted from the earlier, happier moments of our union, little glow bug personalities, a girl and a boy, aged at this current time fifteen and thirteen, old enough to know which end is up, the shape of the world, which side of their toast is buttered. Who left whom.

The departure was not a complete surprise. For some months, she had been busy recalibrating her various personal gyroscopes through the steadying and edifying effects of psychological counseling and two tiny tabs of daily Zoloft. She often patted herself on the back for her newfound clarity and strength, pharmaceutically based as it might have been. And yet, her leaving struck me with the unexpectedness of a disease. I shambled about for months not unlike a career sailor home after a long stint at sea. The world continuously shifted beneath my feet, and I found myself unable to locate ground that wasn't rolling and tumbling.

Hence, I quit ambulating altogether and took to the only chair left in my echoey sunroom, replaying my mistakes and sipping on libations Brian brought to me after he ended his shift at the Michelin plant, where he inspects tires for defects and possesses the daily burden and personal responsibility of shutting down the entire North American assembly line at the mere sight of a misplaced rubber pimple.

At my lowest depths, when I found myself asking (actually, begging) her to return and give me/us/it another go, I also discovered an important fact: There was an actor who was left off the original cast list in this drama. It was a man whom, at that time, I wouldn't have known had he walked into my house and sat beside Brian on what I have come to learn is called a *settee*. Bottom line? She already had a man-in-hand, so to speak, when she left. Which may be why she didn't cry as she pulled down the driveway, mangling second gear.

At this time, Brian will pour us a second plastic tumbler of Evan Williams. Evan Williams is only passable bourbon, slightly oaky, drunk by those who secretly aspire to Booker's or Blanton's or the finer roster of brown liquors. Brian and I drink Evan Williams because our fathers drank Evan Williams, and while we have no great yearning to duplicate the meandering footsteps of those from whose loins we have sprung, we enjoy swimming in the eighty-six proof gene pools bequeathed to us by our fathers. It connects us to them. As they have both passed on, we automatically and inadvertently toast them with each semi-smooth sip.

Brian will pour, and we shall pause momentarily in our backpedaling.

?

More background: The man, The Mysterious Other Man, became much less mysterious because of the information offered up by his estranged wife.

Ah, a plot thickener, Brian will say.

Yes, it seems that the mystery man's wife, too, had fled their own domestic dilemma a month prior to my spouse's sprint toward greener grass. She had long suspected her hubby was wading in the murky shallows of an extra-marital encounter, and she substantiated her intuitional stirrings through the uncovering of things: lovey-dovey notes in his briefcase listing times when the two passion birds could meet in convenience store parking lots; whispered reports from the Neighborhood Watch mavens about strange cars overnighting in strange driveways; his cell phone records detailing the interesting calls at uninteresting times from my one and only.

The final punch in her exit chit was the time she heard him behind a closed door, leaving a rather long and detailed phone message on someone's voicemail. Moments later, she found his cell phone and fingered the redial button. My lovely's name and cell number appeared on the little screen.

Ah, technology, I whisper.

Ah, Brian will say, *stupidity*.

How do I know all of this? I found out through the passage of time and the Darwinian evolution of information. That is to say, the strongest bits of information always survive for impending discovery. And, of course, time eats its own tail. That is also to say, some of this I've come to discover in a less-than-linear fashion and have reconstructed a more rational timeline for your benefit.

She—his wife—finally acted upon her discoveries, packing up her things over the course of a lonely weekend when her husband was away, loading up her furniture (including the expensive ceiling fans she had recently purchased), and making quiet tracks back to the roots of her childhood, to the North Florida town where her parents still lived—happily, it seemed, after forty-seven years of varying bliss.

Brian will caution me to actually get to a freaking point. He will warn me that I am confusing you and in danger of losing your interest. Brian believes in the simplicity of things. He wants a direct line between A and B, followed thereupon by an unfolding of the rest of the alphabet, in order.

For the sake of simplicity and Brian's Job-like patience, I will now recap in the most efficient manner possible by simply saying: Long before my wife made her dramatic exit, she was bone-smuggling another man while living under the broad umbrella of our marriage. But she minivanned it one hot Sunday afternoon. The Other Man's Wife left him almost simultaneously. The two lovers suddenly found themselves estranged and free to share their passions.

Once we began to live apart, when my children were not with their mother (which was every other week), The Other Man was omnipresent at her new address because, as Brian will surely comment, *that woman you married can't stand to be alone.*

?

Background in a higher gear: After several months of estrangement, the Wife of the Other Guy surprised me with a phone call. Ta da. A shot from the blue, it was. She requested a meeting. She had questions, she said.

I told her my life had also become full of interrogatives. I told her I had actually begun to embody the actual physical shape of the question mark, bent forward like a man with the weight of his world balanced on his collarbones. She didn't comment, unfazed by my emotion or spinal condition, but she did say she had specific things to ask me and requested I meet her in a neighboring town where she had traveled for work.

Brian believes this: the Wife of the Other Guy was on the prowl for what Brian calls "the revenge screw." The ultimate payback, he called it. Doing the Other Woman's Man. While it is an interesting cultural concept, I did not agree with Brian's analysis. I had heard the woman on the phone. She sounded wounded, not predatory.

I realized it was clearly the wrong thing to do, to see this woman, who, like her husband, was a ghost to me, a face I could not have picked out of a small crowd. Yet, I was insanely interested. And was I curious?

Brian will no doubt counter: *Is he curious?! Hell, does a shark have a watertight asshole?*

?

So, the encounter. Picture me at a six-stool, waiting-for-your-table bar in a small restaurant. I was indeed passing time, with a tumbler of house bourbon and water. This establishment did not stock Evan. It occurred to me that I had been stood up. Then the door opened, and a woman walked through it. She was pretty from the shoulders up, brown hair, streaked with highlights. A nice face, a soft face, edged with heartache. I was immediately enthralled with her—not in a romantic, here's-my-room-key sense, but attraction as in the wanting-to-make-her-hurt-less sense.

She sounded urgent and in pain on the phone, and, at first blush, she seemed too nice to be on, as Brian will say, the shit end of anyone's stick. She had dressed for this meeting. A sleeveless, light sweater and hoop earrings too large for her face. She asked if I was me, and I said I was indeed, and we were shown to our table by the chain-smoking man who owned the restaurant. Through his personal fogbank of cigarette smoke, he gave us a look as if to say: *Here is the darkest table I have, you lovers you. Enjoy your shadows.*

At this point, the evening became Dali-esque. The clocks melted. Ice cubes spoke to me. The flatware began to spiral and pick up radio stations. I was transported to another world where information was the sole currency. Strangeness ensued. The chit chat I will leave to your imagination. She finally said she had two questions for me, which I will relate precisely as she asked them, in all their bizarreness:

Question #1—"Did your wife like to be with other women?"

Question #2—"Did you and your wife ever go to swinger parties?"

Brian will now beg me to leave the background and insert some forward-moving action into this tale, which I will do, after we both sip from the Brown Fount of Evan.

?

Recent history, not background: Last night, Brian and I walked into our local watering hole, an oyster bar that no longer served seafood of any type, much less oysters, but maintained the old-salt atmosphere, with wooden lobster traps and tangled seine nets nailed to the walls and bathrooms that were gender-designated as one for the *Gulls* and one for the *Buoys*. Brian and I drink here because we can. We always order Captain Evan Williams neat. We often drink to the point of losing our compass headings, ending up dazed and shipwrecked on the floor of the *Gulls* bathroom.

Last night, we were sipping and content, happy to feel the warmness trickle down our throats toward our toes. Brian and I had reached the advanced state of evolution when we no longer drank for the pleasure of the act, no longer for the lubrication of our social facilities. We drank, as Brian will say, *for the inevitability of inebriation.* Our goal was amiable drunkenness and maintenance of such, and with the perseverance of old-school postal workers, we shant be thwarted as we completed our numerous rounds.

Brian began a story he swore was funny, and I knew would be long—a tale concerning a large chicken truck he had seen that afternoon and a daring, renegade chicken that escaped from his crate of death. Just as he approached a crucial plot point in the chicken story, a man shouldered his way onto the empty stool next to me. This interloper was considerably shorter than I was, but a wide man, solid you might say, solid in the if-he-fainted-you-would-hate-to-be-tasked-with-breaking-his-fall manner.

He ordered a light beer and Brian sneered. (Brian thinks our world has been hastened toward an earlier-than-scheduled Armageddon because of the proliferation of "light" products, but I will avoid this tangent. Suffice it to say, reduced fat mayonnaise pisses him off.)

The solid man looked up at me and spoke, and this frightened me. I am cautious of making conversation with strangers. Brian is much better at shooting the proverbial breeze with barflies, yet he would never converse with a light beer drinker. When the man's mouth opened, I could tell that his evening of consumption began hours ago, probably while the sun still shone. His tongue had a mind of its own. His words floated into the air, their syllables stretching like salt water taffy. I sensed he was the kind of man who found intestinal fortitude in a bottle of low-calorie beer.

"You don't know who the fuck I am, do you?" he slurred, and a smile wiggled across his face.

"Correct," I said, trying not to look down upon him. But I did anyway. His hair was thinning at the topmost twirl. I spun Evan in my short glass. I wanted one of us to walk away. I considered making a trip to the *Buoys* room.

"Well, I know you, sport," he re-slurred, waving his finger in the demilitarized zone of my personal space. I felt Brian bristle and move slightly toward the light beer connoisseur, who continued. "I know so much about you, it would scare you, man. I can't believe you don't know who the fuck I am. That's almost disrespectable. I know you. And you know what? You shouldn't ought to have done it."

The word *it* was so...so gauzy. I had no idea what *it* was, and to find out required me asking a question. I mulled the idea of speaking. Then Brian—always quiet, always observant Brian—noticed a distinctive outline through the shirt of the stranger, just at nipple height. And the shirt, Brian will also mention to you later, was silk and loudly colored, like a tourist's, which we both agree worked well with the ex-oyster bar décor.

?

Back to background: Which takes us back to the table in the Italian ristorante.

I ordered the all-meat kabob (spicy Italian sausage, beef, and pork linked with grilled peppers), her the salmon. She pronounced the "el" in *salmon*, which Brian will consider some sort of gene marker for lack of classical education, until I remind him that many people mispronounce food words and that fact never diminishes the enjoyment of their entrée. I even know a rich, powerful man who cannot pronounce the word *idea*. Instead, he always comes up with good *ideers* that make him more money.

I answered both of her interrogatives with the negative. My wife had never exhibited bi-sexual tendencies. Brian will, of course, huff that every man's fantasy is the traditional ménage for three; however, while that pay-per-view thought might have flickered momentarily across my dreamscape during seventeen years of marriage, it was an urge never mentioned, much less acted upon. And as for the subject of swinging, I had never been intrigued by the allure of a roomful of strange skin, and I don't think my wife was either. No. And no.

The woman across the table seemed disappointed. "Rats. It would have explained a lot," she said, holding her fork like a pencil, awaiting her salmon. She paused, but I could think of nothing to say, so I resorted to the classic Repetition Strategy With Ascending Intonation.

"A lot?" I echoed.

And, hereupon, she launched. She catapulted. She grabbed the zipline of narration and stepped off the safety of the cliff's ledge, reeling off a story that was interrupted only by her need for oxygen intake and the quiet appearance of the waiter at our tableside, who delivered her grilled salmon and my kabob, refilled our glasses, then ducked into the shadows near the espresso machine.

Much in the manner of a court reporter, I will now relate her words as best as I can recollect them:

About two years ago or maybe two and a half—oh lord, I can't remember specifically because things begin to run together after a while, but I can remember which order they came in, that's for sure—he came home at the end of one day and lifted up his shirt and showed me his new pierced nipple, and I said, What in the world is that there for? I was shocked. Wouldn't you be? It looked like it hurt. And he said it was something he'd always wanted to do and he just decided to do it, just that afternoon, just like that. Now, is that unusual or what? How many men just decide one day to get their nipple pierced? Don't you talk about these things first? I told him he couldn't show it to our daughters. I was afraid it would scare them, seeing their daddy's nipple pierced.

Interjection: The Other Man and his pained wife have two young children, younger than my two. Our two. The two I've already mentioned. Brian will chide me for leaving out this detail earlier.

He seemed a little miffed when I said not to show the girls, but he agreed. Then, a couple of months later, he came home with a Prince Albert.

I simply must tell you my reaction at this point. I had none. She said *he came home with a Prince Albert* the same way she might have said he arrived at the front door with a carton of eggs. Prince Albert? In the can? Prince Albert hinted at tobacco and pipe smoking. A man pierces his nipple and begins to smoke a pipe? Yes, that is strange but not cause to commit one to an asylum. Brian will snicker because of my lack of cultural acumen.

I said nothing and must have had a rather bland look across my forehead. She noticed my lack of brain activity.

You don't have any idea in the world what I'm talking about, do you? Well, I suppose it's safe to say that I didn't have any idea what a Prince Albert was back then, either. I hear some people call it a PA. But what it is, is—and I'm almost embarrassed to say, well, I'm very, very embarrassed to say, so you'll have to excuse me—is a type of penis piercing, yes, that's right, a piercing done to the penis, right through the end, the hole, you know, whatever the name of that hole is, the u-something, and then back through the back side sort of. The thing—I don't mean THE thing, but the metal thing that goes through the holes—is sort of horseshoe-shaped and has little tiny balls you screw onto the end, to keep it from sliding out, I suppose. It's very intimidating to look at, if you were to see one. Well, this of course put me right over the edge. During the few weeks while he was waiting for the thing to heal, he was urinating blood. God, it was awful, but he was so happy with his Prince Albert, even with the blood in the toilet. Did you know that because you have a new little hole, you actually pee from, well, from two holes? I never knew any of this, any of this at all. So, that was the beginning of it. First, the nipple. Then the other thing. The Prince Albert. I'm sorry to tell you this. I know this isn't what you expected, was it?

Expectations. The expected unexpected. The improbable possible. You would expect my jaw to drop, wouldn't you? Perhaps expect the blood to rush from my head. Instead, I simply looked down. There, on the plate, was my kabob, the ends of the wooden skewer charred a little after it pierced the sausages and the steak. I shivered at the synchronicity of it all. It seemed suddenly humorous: My wife, rubbing up against Prince Albert, rubbing up against, as Brian will say, *A man with a Christmas ornament on the end of his wang doodle.*

I wanted to laugh, but I knew that was not the reaction she wanted. I felt a bit like crying as well. In lieu of either, however, I spoke across the table.

"The beginning, you said? The beginning of it?" I repeated, again exercising the ol' Echo and Intonate Technique.

Whereupon, she leaned on the accelerator of her story and proceeded to tell me what she called, cutely, the *flurry of red flags*, all of which will wave for you in due time, but only after more from the oyster bar.

?

Brian will say I think too much, and I admit contemplation has cost me as much in bad timing as it has helped me gain a mental advantage, but I stood at the bar, wondering if this solid, smallish man was searching for a fight. All the signs were readily apparent: irrational bullying, the inability to reason quickly, too much beer. Not that I would run to avoid a fight. I know the sensation of someone's teeth crumbling like Chiclets against my knuckles. I have spread a man's nose with a forehead butt. I may not look like a fighter, but that makes me a dangerous man. I'm constantly camouflaged. Brian will say that sometimes that decent bourbon goes to my fists as much as my head. I will not argue with him.

However, I was not about to violate rule #1 of bar fighting, which is: Don't Fight in the Bar.

There are too many sharp edges in a bar, too many table corners, too many chair legs, too many witnesses, too many weapons within reach (e.g., bottles, rings of keys, cell phones—yes, a smartphone in an open palm directly to the temple can bring a strong man to his knees. Ask Brian.) Hence, I turned away, turned to go, which means I failed to see the nipple piercing straining against the fabric of his Hawaiian shirt. Had I seen it, I might have begun to put two and two together. But Brian is much better at that. He reads Sherlock Holmes for fun in the evenings.

And yet, this man in a very loud shirt followed me, nipping at my heels as I weaved through tables topped with small seashells buried in a thick coating of clear shellac. Brian wondered who was paying our tab, but I was too intent on getting into the darkness, into the air, where perhaps I could reason with this small man who insisted he knew me, where I might be able to ask what *it* was.

He said things to me as we made our way through the bar: "I know you well enough to know you'd be here." And: "You shoulda thought more about it before you did it." To which I wanted to reply that I thought too much as it was. And just as I cleared the doorway into the parking lot, he said: "You can't believe everything my ex-wife tells you, you stupid fuck. That bitch is crazy."

Ah, yes. And Brian will tell you without hesitation at that precise second, I turned and, in the backlight of the open door, I saw the small wide man, the Other Man, standing there in his Hawaiian shirt and his nipple ring, grinning at me like he was the more intelligent of us because he knew what I'd been doing and to whom I'd been talking and, in that instant, I vowed not to violate rule #2 of bar fighting: Never Throw the First Punch.

And I didn't, even when he said: "You ought not to have written that story, you ass wipe."

?

I had truly hoped to get through this retelling without regurgitating the entire episode about the short story.

Unavoidable, Brian will say.

And he is correct. Once the story was published, I should have expected some sort of recoil and reaction. I will explain quickly. This particular section isn't really background. It's fiction. But not really.

Some months ago, I wrote and typed up a short story about a woman who tells her children and her husband that she is going to the nearby coast for a weekend to clear her head, whatever that means.

To make a short story shorter, the wife actually spends a weekend—quite on the sly—halfway across the country, in Texas with her lover, sipping margaritas and eating San Antonio's finest riverside burritos. Quite by accident, the husband finds out about his wife's Lone Star interlude and that she has lied to a number of friends and family, and he thinks about what to tell the two children, both of whom ask why Mommy didn't leave a phone number or name of a hotel on the coast to which she never traveled. "Can we call her?" they ask early in the story.

At the end of the tale, he sits his little glow bug children down and begins to tell them where/how their mother is actually spending the weekend to clear her head. The last line was probably the only good line in the whole story: *He was a man never comfortable throwing a first punch.*

I cannot truthfully tell you why the story made its way into the editorial pipelines. Automatic writerly reflex, I suppose. Write, rewrite, send out. Natural urge. Cheap therapy, perhaps. To my surprise, the story was taken immediately by a small literary magazine with a readership that could fit comfortably into a mid-sized sedan. The editor asked if they might print the tale in their summer issue. Brian will say that he cautioned me to refuse their offer of publication, but upon careful thought I decided, *What could it hurt?* Brian will say I didn't plan on the Other Man being a literature aficionado and invading our oyster bar, and he is right as rain.

The things you don't see coming. They will leave teeth marks on your ass.

?

The flurry of red flags. More information from the Other Wife in the restaurant:

He started to make me look at places on the Internet, sites about parties for swingers, and he would say, 'We should try that' or 'Haven't you ever wondered?' And you won't believe this: If I had to leave town on business, he would beg me to pick up somebody on the road and sleep with this person and then come home and tell him about it. I never did that, I mean, he was the first person I ever slept with, we met in college for god's sake and now he's asking me to pick up men? Once he even asked me to bring somebody home and have relations with this person so he could watch from the closet. You're wondering why I didn't leave him, aren't you? Well, you never think the worst, do you? You always think: this is a phase or this will pass. It's an early middle-age crisis or an urge he never got to act on when he was a teenager or maybe it's something that happened when he was little because, you know, he always told me that his brother was abused by this uncle I'd never met and that got me to thinking, I can tell you that. I mean, who knows who really got abused? I mean, people are always talking about how that messes them up forever.

He would do crazy things. He emptied all of the garbage from the house into the trunk of my car when he thought I threw away his pack of chewing tobacco. Yes, he chews tobacco. It makes his bottom teeth brown. Garbage in the trunk of my Subaru. No, I'm not making this up. I can't make things up. I tried to make up stories about picking up men when I traveled out of town because if I didn't, he would get all mad and all. But I can't make up stories like that. I'm not creative. So when I found out that your wife was the one, at least the one I knew about, I decided to leave. One weekend while he was away at some conference in Texas, I got the neighbors to help me pack everything up and we left. They say I stole his thunder. Plus, I never did any of the crazy sex things he asked me to. That's something to hold onto, I guess, right?

?

At the threshold of the oyster bar, questions sprinted through my brain. What could I say to this man with the bespangled nipple, not to mention bespangled pecker, that wouldn't sound like a third-grade playground retort? *You're not the boss of me? I know I am but what are you?* Because the fact of the matter was, I wrote the story. And maybe I shouldn't have done it. But that was ink under the bridge, so to speak. I would never have pictured him as the kind of man who read obscure literary magazines.

But, to be honest, he did not wait for my reply. Rather, he stepped out of the dull bloom of light from the oyster bar and said: "You want some more material, motherfucker? Let me show you some of the things your wife is up to these days. I've even got pictures, sport."

If you're a connoisseur of bar fighting, that is a cue. When he reached for his back pocket and turned his head slightly to follow the path of his hand, I knew my moment had come. And yes, Brian will say that I threw the first punch, but I considered his implication that he had photographic evidence of my wife—okay, ex-wife—and her encounters with Prince Albert a figurative punch of the first degree because, quite frankly, I felt his words in my gut and perhaps even in my head. At that precise second, I saw white light and shooting stars and heard the adrenaline rising in the floodplain of my ears, and so, while one of his hands dug in his back pocket and the other searched for the porch rail of the oyster bar (a rail that is decorated with rope spiraled and glued to the wooden surface), I hit him somewhere in the vicinity of the left ear with my open palm, and he dropped like a tossed duffel bag.

Rule #3 of bar fighting: If At All Possible, Never Hit With Knuckles. Use the open hand or a handy implement. Knuckles have an inherent design flaw, as they break easily when wielded as a weapon.

?

Here was how I felt sitting at the restaurant with his estranged spouse: I felt as if the two of us were in the midst of an extremely difficult 1000-piece puzzle.

Instead of plates littered with salmon remnants and uneaten kabob (I couldn't bear to pull hunks of meat from the wooden skewers after she'd related the Prince Albert story), there was a puzzle on the table and each of us had missing pieces the other wanted and needed. After three hours, we had managed to complete the easy sections—the corners and the edges—and we had enough pieces together to form a recognizable image. We could probably fill in the rest on our own.

The restaurant was empty and quiet and somehow darker, and our waiter had fled once I paid the check and his tip. Neither of us had ordered dessert, though she had the waiter recite the possibilities, as if she were receiving some vicarious pleasure just from hearing the words *key lime* and *tiramisu*.

I waited (with Brian's early cautions still hissing in my ear) for her to turn the worm and ask me back to the Hampton Inn or Embassy Suites, so she could show me several of the things she had witnessed during her Internet excursions. We had talked in terms so personal, my ears warmed. We had consumed wine, but, to her credit, she was only after information. Puzzle pieces.

We walked out of the restaurant and said goodbye to the owner, who sat at the bar, poring over receipts, waving to us through the cumulus fog of his cigarettes. He winked at me.

It occurred to me to ask the Next Question, to see if she would be interested in a nightcap in an even darker locale. I thought revenge might take that form for me as well. But just outside the door, our waiter stood, now dressed in jeans and a t-shirt, wringing his hands, juvenile-style, near his car, a Geo with the hood up like an open mouth.

"You got any jumper cables I could borrow?" he asked me before I could avoid him. "I'm totally dead." And his question took the air out of my mood.

?

Though I tend to think more about things than he does, Brian possesses a much quicker brain. He didn't suspect anyone actually saw me cold cock Nipple Ringer, which was why Brian immediately yelled back through the door of the oyster bar, something to the effect that our friend had one too many. We struggled to pick him up off the porch, and I immediately questioned what we were going to do with him. Brian said to drag him to my car, which sat in the dark, gravel parking lot.

Prince Albert Guy was semi-conscious, his legs moving only by the momentum of some distant muscle memory. We found my beat-up Saab at the edge of the lot, next to a chain-link fence. I didn't remember leaving it there, but Brian assured me that this car was mine. It possessed all the birthmarks—the headliner drooped and the left-front rim was missing.

I left the engine off but turned on the headlights. We laid him in the dirt in front of the car, and he began to roll a bit in the light, and I needed time to think, so I did indeed violate rule #4 of bar fighting: Never Hit a Man While He's Down.

Which was to say, I popped him another quick one to the temple to send him back to Comaville because, quite frankly, I didn't want to listen to him anymore.

Once he lapsed into paralysis, Brian and I both saw that the Other Man had wet himself, which seemed a small, disgusting, possibly sarcastic act, and I was about to roll him onto his stomach when Brian told me to wait and he, Brian that is, did something that I will admit I was contemplating, but would have never attempted. Brian unzipped the guy's fly. Brian then looked at me and commented that I wanted to see it as badly as he did because the only time we've ever seen a PA was in bad photos on the Internet following that dinner with this very man's ex-wife, pictures that were painful to witness.

Brian may tell you that he didn't have to persuade me to continue with the unveiling, but, call me weak-stomached, I truly had no desire to dig through piss-soaked boxer shorts in search of Prince Albert. Brian, however, was a fearless, single-minded explorer, and with a quick push and grab, he uncovered the penis of the man in the dirt and there, in the glare of the headlights, was Prince Albert, gold and shining, lying in its wrinkled background of tartan boxer material, its u-shape cutting through the end of its owner's Johnson like half a smile.

As I wondered at its very existence, Brian clamored into the back of my car and suddenly asked aloud if I still had my jumper cables.

"Jumper cables?" I answered, instinctively utilizing the Echo and Repeat Strategy.

Brian was mad. But not at me. I had no grasp of the depths of his anger, his sudden fixation on exacting lasting revenge because—and this was a completely novel idea to me—Brian wanted to clamp one end of the jumper cable to the Prince Albert and the other to the car's battery, spin the engine, and blow the Other Man's Penis into its most elemental elements. He wanted revenge as bad as I did. He's that kind of friend.

When I reminded Brian that this would more than likely kill him, Brian said something that sounded like, *Yeah? So?*

And before I could retain my bearings, Brian popped the hood, connected positive to positive and negative to negative, and headed for Prince Albert with the jumper cable in his hand, wondering aloud if he should have ground the extra negative connection to the engine block.

Brian clamped the jumper cable to the ball-end of the Prince Albert. While this could have ultimately been a sight to treasure and hold dear, I could not allow it. I unclamped the cable from the battery of my Saab, so all was well and safe once more, and, to be quite honest, Brian suddenly regained a measure of sanity as he gazed at a man with a battery cable on his penis. Brian shook his head and conceded the more contemplative of us should probably take over.

Which I did. Once the Other Man was completely unhooked, I reached into his back pocket and there, just like he threatened, I found amateurish photos of him and my ex-wife engaging in various forms of Ultimate Bump and Grind, grinning at the camera, their various piercings catching and reflecting light. (Ah, yes, another puzzle piece floated into place. My former wife had her belly button pierced not long after she fled in the minivan. She and our eldest received a two-for-one special at a local parlor. Piercings. Common bonds. Ah, a mother's love.) I wondered who took the photos. Brian will say they more than likely utilized the camera's timer. Let's hope.

Brian will also say that I stared at the pictures much longer than necessary, that I spent an inordinate amount of time examining my wife in the light of the car, and I will say that he is probably right. But I also say that I was formulating a small plan that we put into action at that very moment. It was simple and somewhat dramatic and overtly visual.

What did I do? I selected what I felt was the most provocative photo of the entire collection and, with my ignition key, made a small hole in its corner, then slid the photo into my shirt pocket.

Brian and I dragged the PA owner toward the porch of the ex-oyster bar, waited until there was no traffic through the door, then placed him in one of the ancient rockers just on the edge of the shadows. I suppose sea captains were known for their ability to rock in a chair.

At this point, Brian and I drew straws and I, of course, lost, which forced me to be the one who unscrewed the small golden ball on one end of the crescent-shaped apparatus, onto which I threaded the hole in the photo. I then re-screwed the ball, and the photo dangled safely on the end of the Other Man's Penis like the flag of an embarrassed country.

Brian will snort that I failed to mention the most important thing, and he would be correct. On the photo, in the white border at the bottom, I wrote in pen:

Call for pick-up, 321-9610.
Woman on the line is familiar with
this pecker.

321-9610 was the cell phone number belonging to my lovely ex-wife. Brian and I walked back into the bar and, after ordering two Evans neat with beer chasers, we loudly mentioned to the bartender that there was some drunk on the porch with his dick hanging out, and what was more, there was a damn picture stuck on the end, a photo of the guy and some woman going at it. The word spread virus-like down the bar. In ninety seconds, the porch was chock full of men with their cell phones to their ears, grinning, trying to connect with the annoyed, confused woman at 321-9610.

?

Brian will pour us another Evan while we sit in my drafty sunroom. On the makeshift coffee table in front of me, the pictures fan out, face up, like a bad poker hand. Brian will say that I should go ahead and do it, that I should send them—at least one of them—to Prince Albert's ex-wife. He will say that she would want to see it.

"Maybe so," I tell him. But I add that perhaps it's one puzzle piece too many. Brian wants to know what any of this has to do with puzzles.

I take a long, oaky sip and tell him to be quiet. I study the pictures of my naked ex-wife and the Prince. "I need time to think," I say to Brian.

He doesn't remember—I'm the one who does the thinking.

Smokey the Bear Has the Matches

TJ drove without lights on. His girl Treecie was all but in his lap, a hand wedged between her legs. Both of them all drunk up or stoned, her worse off than him, which could have been something to take advantage of, but she was relatively safe except for TJ's finger walking up her thigh.

I had out my Blue Tips, those long, strong wooden matches that don't break when you strike on them. I was waiting for TJ to hit the bridge and head back up the bluff and toward the old rundown deer camp above the floodplain.

I heard too many frogs from where I laid back in the lounge chair TJ kept in his truck bed. Big brown ugly dudes. I imagined them sitting white-bellied and proud at the edge of the water, wondering, I bet, what that noise was rattling down the road out there in the dark without lights on. I stuck my nose up. Out there smelled like the inside of a magazine. Jasmine and honeysuckle clouds. If TJ knew I thought about flowers, he would more than likely beat me up.

The hump of the bridge bounced me up in the lounge chair. The truck machine-gunned over the bridge spacers then hit the other side of smooth asphalt. I pulled out a Blue Tip, rolled the working end between my fingers. No shape in the world like the end of a Blue Tip. I stuck it up my nose a little ways. Smelled like a bomb getting ready to go off, like a science class I had back before I told high school adios. Smelled like the end of the damn world as we know it.

TJ slowed down and swung off the paved road, worked the truck into a lower gear. He didn't like driving on dirt because he had to keep shifting when he hit a curve or when he went up the bluff away from the river. Took two hands. I told him one day that he should just get him a truck with an automatic transmission, and that way he wouldn't have to keep pulling his hand out of Treecie's crotch every time the RPMs dropped. He told me to shut up, and that was that.

We reached the swamp. Stunk like a nasty fart that never blew away, hanging in the thick air and tangling up in the trees. We rolled under the tree tunnel that stole the sky away on this part of the road, a little bit of a hill under us, the truck drumming on the washboard ruts. I hummed and listened to my voice vibrate like an old man's. Treecie banged her head against the back window of the truck, and I knew she was fixing to have a big one. The bumps in the road were probably helping him out.

We came up on the first big curve, and TJ let off the gas. He didn't go for the gear shift because Treecie was still banging her head against the back window and flopping on the seat like a fish on a dock. The truck lurched from lack of power.

"Shit!" TJ yelled.

"Damn you," Treecie yelled back when his hand reached toward the shifter.

He hunted for second gear and ground some metal trying to find it. The truck caught gear and jumped around the curve. My lounge chair slammed against the side of the truck.

"I'm not done," Treecie whined.

"Told you to get an automatic transmission," I hollered.

Treecie didn't like me much. She slapped the window. "Shut up, you peeping tom."

"You shut up," TJ yelled back to her. "I got another good half mile before I got to shift again." And he went back to where he was, all in and amongst.

We hit another bump, and I dropped my Blue Tip somewhere in the truck bed. I didn't like wasting one of my little disciples like that. Took another from the box and rubbed the end with my middle finger, the magic finger, bird-shooting finger, probably the same finger TJ had on Treecie. I stuck the end of the Blue Tip in my nose again, and Treecie started banging her head against the window. I knew she was coming. Treecie sang the birthday song every time she started to come.

I'd never heard her make it to "Happy birthday, dear..." before she gave out of air.

She had her moment, and TJ drove like a moonshiner, sliding around curves and gunning the engine until I thought it was going to explode. I smelled somebody lighting up a joint. It glowed inside the cab right behind my head. We left out from under the tree tunnel, and we got the stars back. I started counting them and made it to fifty when Treecie knocked on the window. "Hey, you," she yelled.

She had one of her titties pressed up against the window glass like an over-easy egg. I shot her a bird with my magic finger. TJ yelled something I couldn't make out over the wind noise and the cicadas that for some reason had begun to whine in the trees.

We pulled into the old hunt camp, only one building still standing, and it looked like a brown ghost when TJ turned his headlights on it. He walked around to where I was lying in the lounge chair, a bottle in his hand.

"You want you a sip?" he asked.

Treecie walked toward the little hunting shack, her feet padding on the dirt. I reminded him I didn't do hard liquor.

"Well, we just gonna drink it up all ourselves, unless you help," TJ said.

"You going inside?" I asked.

"Yep. I got her all revved up. Time to have my own fun."

"I'll be out here," I said.

"Well, a course you will." TJ smiled. "Doing what you do."

"C'mon, TJ," Treecie yelled from the porch of the building. "I don't have all night. I have to get home."

"Like anybody's worried where you are," TJ said under his breath. When TJ walked on the porch, I could see how little Treecie was standing next to him. He ain't changed his whole life. He's always been tall and thick and strong enough to live forever. Treecie was tiny and mean like those little dogs nobody likes, but everybody has got one of.

"Hey, turn off the truck lights," Treecie screamed at me. "We don't want a dead battery."

I left them in the dark in the building where there wasn't anything but a mattress and a flashlight and a roll of paper towels for cleaning up. TJ didn't want an accident. Treecie's husband would probably wonder what baker it was who stuck a bun up his wife's oven.

I laid my Blue Tips on the side rail of the truck. Daddy's little soldiers. The mosquitoes found me. They buzzed my ears and lit on my hands and on that pulsing place on my ankle. They were going crazy, sniffing out blood. I finger-rolled Blue Tip number one, then stood it up on the launch pad, the bomb end against the striker and the other end pressed hard against my fingertip. Then I flicked with my other finger. The match sailed through the air like fireworks and landed fifteen feet off in the woods, in among the pine straw. Flick flash fly. Again and again. I imagined the ants on the ground watching the balls of fire dripping from their sky. I was god, raining down hellfire and brimstone on the ant world. I was vengeful and spiteful. They'd learn. One day, they'd learn. I was a feared man in the ant world.

Fifteen minutes later, I was out of matches, and Treecie and TJ walked up to the truck, scaring me. I was off somewhere else, in my head. Treecie laughed, "Earth to idiot…did you miss us?"

"Stop teasing him," TJ said. Treecie stuck out her tongue.

I looked around the truck at the brush under the trees. I saw a few of my little soldiers working away brightly on their own. My little disciples. Spreading the word of the vengeful god. Bringing vengeful news. I could feel a hundred mosquito bites on my body. Blood of my blood.

"My work here is done," I said. "Let us go forth." Treecie rolled her eyes and climbed in the driver's side, then slid over and waited for TJ.

?

The judge floated in like he was flying, flew right into his chair, his black coat trailing wings behind him. He started in on me.

"Now, you, young man, are telling this court that you indeed deliberately set these fires, that you wantonly and maliciously burned up a hundred and twenty acres of my county?"

He stopped, and I kept my mouth closed.

"Don't let me put words into your mouth, son. Truth be told, what you are saying is absolutely *nothing*. Is that correct? You aren't saying you did, but you aren't saying you didn't either."

The judge mixed his eyebrows together with his fingers. The whole room was the brown color of weak chocolate and almost empty. No TJ. Of course, no Treecie. A couple of old people, who didn't seem as lonely here as they would out on the street, sat on the back row. One of them had a sandwich in a plastic bag.

"Mr. Lawrence?" The judge spoke to the table across from me, where a man sat with a bored expression that fit him better than his suit.

"Yes, Your Honor?"

"Let me tell you what we got. Since you are the only lawyer here, I'll talk to you. This human over here isn't talking."

"Yes, Your Honor."

"What I have here, Mr. Lawrence, as you may or may not be well aware, is that this young man is accused of setting the fire. Arson. He isn't talking, though. There is no evidence he set the fire other than the fact that he was in a pickup at some point near the scene of the conflagration. He is not denying his complicity in the crime. I have a woman who swears on the graves of her unborn children that this mute set the fire. This woman, who upon first examination seems quite upstanding, may in fact be of dubious character and wishes to remain anonymous because she was actually at the scene throwing off sparks of her own with another gentleman, who is the pickup's owner. In a separate affidavit, the gentleman with the pickup swears on the graves of his paramour's unborn progeny that this young man did not—I repeat, did not—set any fire of any kind. This gentleman is quite willing to appear in front of me and testify to this fact. Whereas the woman, hoping to keep her spouse from discovering her nocturnal dalliances, is doing everything possible to keep out of a public venue. Have I got this correct so far, Mr. Lawrence? Am I telling you anything you do not already know?"

"Yes, Your Honor. I mean, no, Your Honor." Mr. Lawrence shuffled around inside a suit so big on him, the cloth didn't move.

"To continue—and don't you go eating in my courtroom, you hear me, Gladys?"

The woman in the back had that sandwich out. Egg salad, I think it looked like, smeared across the side of her mouth. I made a little motion with my hand, a little signal to tell her she had something hanging onto her face, and she smiled back at me. She saw me and wiped with the back of her hand. Then she shoved that sandwich into the bag and mumbled something at the judge he couldn't hear.

"Now, Mr. Lawrence, I have a dilemma. I personally think that side of the river where the fire occurred needed a good burning to clear out the underbrush and make the quail hunting a little better next fall. But what I think doesn't amount to a hill of legal beans. You, sir, have no physical evidence. Your circumstantial evidence is about as thin as the smoke from this fire we're talking about. I can't really put much faith in the testimony of your witnesses. What am I to do, Mr. Lawrence?"

The way he worked those eyebrows with his fingers, it was a wonder he had any hair left in them. I could tell the judge was having trouble coming to a decision. I wanted to open my mouth, but TJ had told me not to say anything unless I absolutely had to. And cry if you can, he told me.

"Your Honor?"

"Yes, Mr. Lawrence?"

"The county would be quite happy with some sort of community service arrangement that would—"

"Mr. Lawrence, sir, you are a mind reader. A medium. Exactly what I was thinking myself. You could have a career telling fortunes long after the law is done with you."

"Yes, Your Honor."

"Here's what I propose. I have a brother-in-law who works for the state, an employment decision that succinctly illustrates his mental powers. He is a forester. A tree hugger. In addition to his many useless duties, he is in charge of the Smokey the Bear costume, and, as I well know, he searches constantly for some poor soul to assume the identity and character of Smokey for various public functions, such as visits to schools, holiday parades, and the like. That, my amateur Prometheus..."

The judge cut his eyes to me.

"That is your debt to be paid in full to society. You will be Smokey the Bear for the period of one year for any and all occasions that the great Bear's appearance is needed. Should you ever refuse to put on the fur and hat, I shall toss you into the county jail for a term up to, but not exceeding, twelve months, and jail is a place where no good mother's son should ever set foot, where men are stacked like pasteurized cheese slices. You shall report to my brother-in-law Monday morning bright and early to get your appearance schedule, and, sir, there is no hibernation period for Smokey the Bear. He works the year 'round. Gladys, let's break for lunch, okay dear?"

?

I never told TJ and Treecie what my sentence was, never told them I had to wear a bear suit. It was all too sad to talk about. I stopped riding in the back of the truck. They broke up a few weeks after I started being Smokey the Bear. TJ said they had a big fight out at the deer camp, and she ended up walking all the way to town on foot, through the swamp and bugs, in the middle of the night.

He told me this over the phone. TJ was one of the few men I'd ever known who liked talking on the phone. He said he couldn't be seen with me for a while. "You and them matches of yours got me this close to a felony-type thing. I could've been in big trouble because of you. How'd you stay out of jail?"

I told him I was on probation and had to do community service, but I didn't say a thing about the Smokey suit. Nobody knew it was me wearing that heavy thing. That was the way I wanted it. I wasn't embarrassed by it. I just wanted a secret I could keep, wanted something nobody else had.

He gave me the story. "We come out to the hunt camp like usual and she says, *TJ, we aren't going anywhere*, and I say, 'Where you want to go, the truck's got plenty of gas,' and she says, *You don't understand. We aren't going anywhere in this relationship*, and I told her something like, 'You been watching television again with your husband and thinking those shows are real life?' And she hit me right in the mouth."

"No, she didn't."

"Sure enough." He seemed proud of it.

"Where did she want to go?" I asked him.

"She said she wanted to go and grow. Wanted us to *go* forward and *grow* into something meaningful," TJ said.

"She make that up?"

"No. Like I said, I think she saw it on TV."

"Or read it in a magazine," I offered up.

TJ paused, then said, "I hadn't thought of that."

"So she walked across the swamp?"

"Yep."

"At night?"

"Yep."

"But you were following along with the truck, right?" I said.

"Nope." He seemed proud again.

"I'd call that impressive," I said. "I'm guessing you're all broke up?"

"You mean, am I sad?" TJ said.

"Well, no. I mean, the two of you are official broke up?"

"Ain't even talking, if that tells you something."

"You two never talked all that much anyway." I thought I might be saying too much, stepping over a line, but TJ didn't mind.

"It was purely a sex thing, I realize that," he said.

"She got tired of that, I reckon."

"Fuck you." He bowed up a little, like I'd made fun of him.

"Sorry."

"She wasn't tired of what we was doing. She just wanted something more on top of it. Damn, I got to find me somebody to ride out to the camp with. I got needs."

"Don't we all," I said. And that was the last anybody ever said about Treecie.

?

Then, she came back in a dream. I don't remember anything about the dream except the way I was feeling when I woke up, the dream buzzing in my head like a pissed-off bumblebee. I couldn't shake it. All day long, I thought I would go crazy. I actually jumped up and down with my head cocked to one side so the thought would fall out. But it stayed stuck there, and it was all about Treecie. She took up residence in my mind's eye. She moved right in there.

When it got dark, I put on my Smokey the Bear suit. It had a body made out of heavy cloth and fake brown fur on the outside. And a headpiece—big and hot—the size of a giant pumpkin. They let me keep it at home. I had been in four different Christmas parades and in almost every elementary school in the county. I'd had kids rub my fur and leave chocolate on my fuzzy backside. Most of the time they all just gathered around and tried to figure out who I really was, but the holes I peeked through were so tiny, my own momma wouldn't know it was me inside that suit.

The suit was the warmest thing I'd ever been in. Tonight, even though it was February and all the people were shut up in their houses to keep out the cold, I was sweating bullets inside the fur. I walked by a car parked underneath a streetlight and looked down at the window and saw my reflection, and, I swear, steam puffed out of the side vents in the Smokey suit.

Treecie and her husband lived in one side of a house right in the middle of town, so she had neighbors just on the other side of the wall. The neighbors next door actually owned the house, an old man named McClary and his wife. McClary slept all the time, Treecie said once, and his wife spent most of her time checking his breathing to be sure he was still alive. "If she isn't sure, she pulls an eyelid up," Treecie told us.

In February there wasn't a leaf on the trees, so you could see right through the neighborhoods and into folks' houses. People were already getting ready for bed when I got to Treecie's. I knew her husband wasn't there. Treecie told us once he worked second shift at the BelMar Plant, making rubber lids for the tops of rubber trash cans.

The sweat ran down my eyes because I was working so hard, jogging from tree to tree so nobody would see me. But it was February, and I don't know if you've noticed this, but nobody looks out their windows in the winter, at least not in this part of the country. We hate winter. A dog ran up to me and sniffed my leg and ran away scared when I growled at him. I sounded real.

Treecie sat on her sofa eating something from a bag. She was watching TV. She didn't look so mean anymore. I knew this would happen. I knew she would be different once she got away from TJ. That was just his way, always making people different than they normally were. Hanging with TJ was like wearing a bear suit. You could be whoever you wanted and nobody'd recognize you.

I had my Smokey nose pressed to her window watching and wondering when she would have to go to the bathroom. She never looked toward the window, but while I squatted there watching her, I didn't notice her husband walk in from the other side of the room, right by the window about a foot from my face. He must have switched shifts. He scared me so bad I pissed in my costume, but I was so damp from sweating you couldn't really tell the difference.

I only stayed for a couple more minutes. I just wanted to see where she lived and what she acted like in her own house. She looked a lot softer through the glass.

?

I got no problem with God. He has done things to be awfully proud of. But like everybody else, He has got out of sorts at times. He has set a fire or two in His day. And I am not the kind to give Him credit for every little thing. He might keep you from walking in front of a pickup one night, but if you were to find a five-dollar bill on the sidewalk it probably has more to do with luck than God. God is not the bringer of luck. He's just God.

I'm just saying, it wasn't God's hand in it when I went to Viewmont Elementary School during Fire Safety Week. It was dumbass blind luck. They wanted us to tell the kids about dropping and rolling and not letting themselves get burned up. I didn't have to say a word. I was Smokey, and Smokey never talks in costume.

"You ain't real," said one kid at Viewmont. "They wouldn't let no real bear loose at school."

I growled at him.

"Bears is louder than that and they can run fast as a car. Lemme see you run," he dared me.

I shook my head.

"Hey y'all, this ain't no real bear." He turned to yell at some of his friends on the playground, which gave me a chance to get away. I ducked around the side of the building and came up on the place where the teachers smoked. Just luck. God wasn't steering me. There was a man in a real nice suit jacket, and there was Treecie. They both sucked on cigarettes like condemned people. A little breeze blew their smoke away as soon as it drifted out of their mouths. I never knew she was a teacher. I guess when we were all in the truck, nobody cared what she did for a living.

They saw me walking up in my costume. "Well, well, Smokey," the man said, and I could tell right off he wasn't from around town. "You've come to stomp our fires into submission, I trust?" Sounded like he was from England or somewhere a long way from here.

I didn't say a word. Just looked at Treecie, her trying to figure out who I was. That's what people do when Smokey walks up. She didn't have a clue.

"Ah, the strong, silent, furry type. I value that in a bear," the man said. I didn't like him right away.

The foreigner and Treecie both reached into their pockets for another cigarette. He lit his new one on the old. Treecie dug around for a lighter. Before she found it, I was standing in front of her with a Blue Tip in my paw.

"Smokey carries his own matches?" She stared into my eyeholes. "Who the hell are you?"

I struck the match on my Smokey belt buckle. It popped to life. I hadn't smelled a burning Blue Tip in ten months. I just carried them around for luck or for something to fill my pockets. She lit up and blew her first puff right in my eyeholes. I couldn't tell if she was being mean or if it just happened naturally.

"Smokey, I suggest you get to know Mrs. Witherman," the fancy man said. "She has unlimited energy, you know. The two of you could be in fire prevention cahoots." He liked hearing himself talk. That much I could tell.

"Be quiet, Thomas," Treecie said like she was talking to a kid. I didn't know she was a teacher. I didn't know she was a Witherman either.

"Thank you for the light," she said back to me. I nodded my head. "I sure would like to know what you look like," she said. "Are you a man?"

Treecie didn't sound like herself. Her voice was quieter and, when words came out of her mouth, she sounded like somebody on television. She didn't sound like a woman who flattened a tittie against the window of a truck.

I nodded, then I did something that just came over me. It was the kind of thing that God might have been involved with. It was not luck. I took Treecie's hand—the one with no cigarette—and I held it in my big fake paw and I bent over and kissed it, which meant I stuck my fake Smokey nose against the top of her hand. Treecie turned red.

"Good God, chivalry lives in a bear costume," Thomas said right before he hacked a couple of times.

I turned and walked away because I was scared what would happen next. But all that happened was Treecie yelling, "What's your name?"

I was Smokey, and that's all she needed to know for now.

?

I went crazy over love. That buzzing in my head moved down toward my heart. All those times when I was in the back of that pickup and Treecie was cussing and letting TJ hustle up and down her leg, now I saw that wasn't really her all those nights. It was fakery. It was like she was trying to fool the world for a couple of hours. I suddenly felt sorry for her. And I was crazy. Somebody ought to have locked me up.

Here she was, still married, and I was a bear going after her. One night I snuck through her neighborhood in my Smokey suit and left a big jar of honey on her front porch. I wanted to kiss that hand again, but I couldn't get near her, so I just did other things. One afternoon after it rained, I put the suit on again and walked through the woods to the school parking lot. I stuck my paw in a mud puddle and left a big, brown paw print on the windshield of her car. Funny thing. People would see me walking around the street in my Smokey suit, and they wouldn't say a thing. A cop passed by, but he knew who I was from all those safety talks at schools.

He just waved. I didn't surprise anybody. People have so many things to worry about in life these days, a bear on the sidewalk won't get a second look. People who have a life like that ought to slow down. A full-grown bear walking down the sidewalk ought to catch your eye, I should think.

Some nights, I'd sit in her flower bed in my Smokey suit, filling up my shoes with sweat, watching her and her husband staring at the TV set. Once he tried to kiss her, and she looked at him like he was a person she hadn't laid eyes on in twenty years. I think she laughed at him. He shook his head and left the room.

A raggedy carnival came to town in the early, early spring. I took the head part of my suit in a big plastic grocery bag to the carnival grounds and went to one of those photo booths with my pockets full of quarters. I must have taken about forty pictures of me wearing the Smokey head, just staring at the camera. I kept smiling and changing my face but every picture looked just the same because the head covered everything. I was there for an hour. A little kid pulled back the curtain because I was taking so long, but when he caught sight of me he dropped a big bag of cotton candy, and he ran off yelling for his momma. I ate that cotton candy.

I started sending Treecie those pictures of me in the Smokey head. I left one taped to her car window. I put one in an envelope and mailed it to her at school. I even stuck one on the outside of her bathroom window.

Don't ask me why. I had no ideas about hurting her or taking her to the deer camp or any of that. I was just crazy. I knew I couldn't have her for my own, what with her husband around, and I wasn't about to do anything to him. It wasn't his fault.

And I didn't have any idea what I'd do if she ever saw my face. All I wanted, I suppose, was a chance to see who that other person was, not the one that bitched like a ticked off little dog, but the other one, the Treecie I caught sight of outside the school that day smoking a cigarette. I figured she'd be somebody I'd like. Long as she didn't know it was me inside that head.

?

The day she left me a note was the best day of my life to that point.

It was stuck on the window of her car. She knew I'd be by. Nice lined paper and really neat printing so I wouldn't have any trouble reading it. The note said to meet her that night at eleven o'clock in the alleyway that ran behind her house. There was a date on the top, real big, so I could be sure what night she was talking about. She thanked me for lighting her cigarette that day at school and said she would like to get to know me better. The letter sounded happy, so happy.

All that day I laid around in my house with the lights off, striking matches and blowing them out. My room smelled like the inside of a wood stove. I took an old washcloth and rubbed hard on the dirty spots on the

Smokey suit. It never came into my mind to wear something else. I was Smokey to her, even though I knew she wanted to find out who was behind the face. I wanted to know the same thing about her. Who was Treecie?

I stood in the alleyway a little before eleven, next to a couple of trash cans full of something that smelled like cat piss. I came close to throwing up inside my Smokey head, but it was the only good place to hide. Late March, but still cold out, with air as dry as a bone so nothing was frozen or slippery. We don't ever get much snow. Nobody knows how to walk on ice in this town.

I kept my eye on the back door on her side of the house. Old man McClary came to his back porch and took a pee between the rails, even though he's got an indoor bathroom. Maybe he couldn't make it up the stairs. He spit in the same direction he pissed and went back to his television. Treecie never opened her back door. The cold air snuck through my eyeholes, but the rest of me was like a heater. I had on extra deodorant that night so the sweat wouldn't make me stink. I didn't have a plan. I decided to leave it all up to luck or God.

I watched the door so hard, I didn't hear the pickup at the other end of the alley rolling toward me slow and quiet with no headlights on. Then out of the corner of my ear I heard the gravel crunching. The headlights flashed on and caught me where I was standing. Two big spotlights that blinded me. I tried to run but went straight over the top of the trashcans and whatever was inside spilled out, and the smell flowed over me like an ocean wave, and I started to puke inside my Smokey head, which I knew in a flash I would have to buy now, since I was in the process of ruining it. I couldn't get the damn thing off my head. My arms were pinned down. I felt somebody else try and snatch it away from my shoulders.

"Motherfucker! Who are you?" he huffed out, trying to get my Smokey head in his hands. It could've been Treecie's husband. I wondered how he knew I was in love with his wife. Her husband seemed like a man who didn't give a shit anymore. This was different. This person with a vice grip on my head did give a shit.

Just as the head came off, I turned toward Treecie's house, and she stood on the back porch watching and waiting. McClary peeked through his backdoor window. In the porch light, Treecie looked so little, like she was a kid, her arms wrapped around her against the cold. Then the whole thing stopped. Nothing moved. *This is what dead feels like*, I thought.

When he punched me, I came back to life. The way he hit me, I spun around and there was TJ over the top of me with his hand in the air. His breath came out in fog bursts. He dropped his fist. He pulled me up into some better light.

"Ah, man," he said. He sounded disappointed.

"Yep, it's me," I answered him.

TJ spit one time, got back in his truck, pulled around me where I was lying in the alleyway, and drove off. I waved toward Treecie, but she was gone. McClary was the only one who kept watching until I finally gathered up my fake head and went on home.

?

The judge was not happy with the condition of the Smokey suit. That night in the alley, the head had rolled amongst the smelly stuff that oozed out the trash can. I tried washing it in the big machine at the coin laundry, but all that did was rub the fur away right down to the bare head. It looked like Smokey had gone to prison and got shaved.

He asked me what I had to say for myself. "Silence. Absolutely nothing each and every time he's appeared before this bench, isn't that correct, Mr. Lawrence?"

Lawrence was in the middle of a big swig of coffee.

"Yes, Your Honor," he gargled. "Not a word."

"I think it's time we heard you say something, either in your defense or by way of explanation," the judge said to me.

I could have told him how when I was Smokey, I wasn't really me and I could do things the old me couldn't do. When I was Smokey the Bear I could imagine being a man in love, and I could watch Treecie, and I could come up with ways to get her attention. I could maybe even make her leave her life. And the most important thing was, when I was Smokey, I didn't need Blue Tips for anything but thinking in my room. I didn't need my little disciples to do any fire starting in the swamp. I could have told him this and then said to him, *Judge, the thing you made me do was the perfect thing. I don't need fire anymore. I got Smokey keeping me warm in the world.*

But I didn't say any such thing. I just looked the judge straight in the eye and told him, "I suppose I took things a little too serious."

?

TJ picked me up in his truck at the county work farm when I was through doing my thirty days. He knew I was getting out because he called me a couple of times, telling me he was sorry because when he hit me he didn't know I was Smokey. Told me Treecie had called him out of the blue and asked if he would beat up some guy in a bear suit that was following her around and being creepy, but not in a nice way. He said he sure as shit didn't figure it to be me. It wasn't long after that, Treecie and her husband moved away to someplace where they could be strangers. TJ had a new woman in the front seat now with him, one I hadn't seen before.

"Hey," he said to me when I walked up to the truck. "Your chair is still in the back."

The woman looked older than she probably really was. Her eyes were bright blue but both sunk into a little nest of wrinkles. She was expecting me to be nice to her, I could tell.

"You aren't Treecie, that's for sure," I said.

"You ain't no goddamn Robert Redford," she said back, and I liked her from that second on.

TJ had a box of Blue Tips waiting on me. The big kitchen kind. Full box. There was a blanket in the back too. I wrapped up in it, and TJ headed for the river. The sun was just starting to go down, and the sky behind the work farm was the color of fire. Made me think about the Blue Tips. I took one out of the box and stuck it near my nose and let the bomb smell drift up to my brain.

I didn't have to peek inside the cab to see what was going on. I could tell by the way TJ whined out every gear, what with his shifting hand busy in the fun spots. I was quickly sadder than I had ever been in my whole life. I got tired all the sudden like I was ninety years old. I had lived a whole life in the last few months. I had destroyed part of the world with my disciples. I fell in love with somebody. I had been a bear. Been hurt because of love. Got beat up. Went to jail. The Flying Judge had told me, "Son, you should learn from all this." All I learned was I couldn't do much better than end up back on the same road in the same pickup again, feeling the same bumps under my ass.

The woman hollered in the cab. So did TJ. It was getting dark, but he didn't turn the lights on. Which I thought was a mistake.

TJ stopped at the crossroads to check for trains. Him and the woman reached across the middle of the seat to kiss. She moved her head up and down during the kiss like she was nodding *yes*. I lit a Blue Tip and reached around and tossed it into the cab while it burned. I lit as many as I could as fast as I could. Tossed them forward.

Before they could figure out what was going on, TJ was screaming about his seat being on fire. Stinky smoke filled the cab. He called me every name he could think of, kept his foot on the brake, and tried to find the key to kill the engine. He was fumbling. The new woman fell through her open door onto the cold tracks. She was laughing so hard, tears began to leak from her eyes, and I liked her even more.

Don't ask me why, but I began to feel better about things.

The Smells at Certain Heights

I am four beers into the morning when Lester comes banging on the door and says we got to go eliminate Howard Johnson. He is yelling this, and his mouth is against the screen, so his voice buzzes, and while I got no neighbors in any direction for acres and acres, it doesn't seem right to be standing on my front porch, going on about eliminating somebody.

It takes a good couple of minutes to make my way across the floor. My back has seized up again. There was another phone call early on this morning. The trouble settled below my belt loops. I hung up with Rhoda and reached over for my jeans and there it went, something snatched tight in my back, and now I can't straighten up. I look ninety-nine years old, all bent over, and the only thing I can see when I try to walk is the tops of my shoes. I couldn't climb a roof today if they paid me triple. The beer helps, though, and I had all but forgotten about the pain until Lester runs up on the porch and starts yelling. Rhoda had been calling about money again.

"But not for me," she said. "For the baby."

Before I unlatch the screen, I tell Lester to shut up. Latching a screen door is one of those things I do and don't really understand why I do it. Like shutting the medicine cabinet before I go to bed or drying off between my toes. It makes sense, but then again it doesn't. If somebody wanted in bad enough, all they'd have to do is punch through the screen and reach in. But I still latch it up at night like it's going to keep out anything bad that walks into the front yard. I can barely lift my neck enough to look up at Les. The sun is a bright spotlight behind his head, filling up the air around him. It makes him look even whiter.

Nobody believes me and Lester are twin brothers. We have won bets in bars because we look so different. He is so white he's almost see-through. Looks like he's been dipped in flour except for the red hair he keeps cut like a Marine. I'm the opposite. I got a tan all year long from crawling on roofs, and my hair is the color of old coffee. We were born three minutes apart, but that fact has never been backed up by anything except stories relatives still tell. When we were little and asked Momma where Daddy was or, hell, *who* Daddy was, her answer was to slap the closest kid so we quit wondering out loud.

Lester walks in and says, "Brother, I have become a victim of supply-side economics, brought on by the lax immigration policy of our current administration." He sits on the edge of my recliner. I can't straighten up to see him or the chair, but I hear his jeans sliding down the Naugahyde. Lester talks the way he does because he spends his days locked up in a dark trailer watching CNN. The fact he doesn't see the light of day much adds even more whiteness to him on a regular basis.

"This isn't a good time," I tell him.

"How come you are all crooked like that?" he says back.

Lester has a short memory for things that got nothing to do with him. He doesn't remember how phone calls from Rhoda tend to go straight to my back. Every time I pick up the phone and hear her on the other end of the line, the muscles just over my hips snatch into a vice grip. That broken heart stuff is all bullshit. My pain is down lower, and it started the day she left me and moved into these apartments called Terrapins Crossing. I don't know exactly what a terrapin is or what they're crossing. The day after she left, I couldn't get out of bed for the pain in my back. Nowadays, it comes on regular, every time she's on the phone.

Before I can answer him, Lester remembers. "Ah," he says. "The Rhoda Effect."

"I ain't working today," I tell him.

"I can see," he says. "But your lumbar trouble is fortunate for me. I need you this morning. Plus, you should avoid heights today. The slant isn't good for your back."

Lester doesn't know what's good for me. He's never figured out why I climb ladders and tack down roofing paper. When I am up in the air, above everything, I feel safe from the kind of world that would make a woman move on to a place where terrapins cross. On the roof, I see better. At the end of the day, the second my feet are a rung from solid ground, I feel the world striking at my ankles like a tub full of rattlesnakes. I told Lester once about the feeling I get when I'm working, but I don't think he understands it. He likes his solid earth. His whole business depends on things staying where they are put.

"Howard Johnson," Lester says, "has a little more cooking in that old motel than just lamb curry and that puffy bread. He's competition now, and I'm not sure the marketplace can sustain the two of us."

"What's he know about crank?" I ask. I am not an expert with meth. I have tried it once, and all I got was sores on the inside of my mouth and on my left cheek, so, for me, it was a waste of good energy. But there are enough people who think different than me, enough that Lester could quit driving trucks and start cooking in his little house. Lester was a long-haul trucker for years. That's when he started speeding so he could stay awake, "especially on the boring, straight parts of the interstate in Florida," he said. He knew it was time to quit driving one night when he thought the weigh station was a toll booth, and he rolled up and pitched four quarters at a highway patrolman behind the glass.

They caught him six exits south and suspended his CDL, mostly because he ran off into a soybean field.

A week later, it was fate or whatever. The sheriff's department put on a crystal meth demonstration in the Piggly Wiggly parking lot as a public safety thing, lecturing folks about what all was in it and how to tell if somebody was mixing it up next door in your neighborhood. The parking lot was full of most of the losers in Williamsburg County, bikers and out-of-work tobacco farmers and, yes, a roofer or two I knew. Everybody had little notebooks they'd bought at the Eckerd's, writing down all the information the deputy called out through a microphone. Lester looked over at me about halfway through the show and said, "This will be easier than I thought." As far as I could tell, Lester was the only one who actually kept his notes and put them into practice. He's got follow through, I'll say that.

Two weeks after the meeting at the Piggly Wiggly, Lester was selling out of his back door to a van full of Mexicans who rode up and down I-95. They were doing cash business with the long-haul boys at truck stops and rest areas. Ever since that day he first started selling, Lester's smelled like either sour chocolate milk or ammonia, but with the money he's making, he doesn't care much about personal hygiene.

Lester taps a Camel on his thumbnail a half dozen times then lights it. He can't smoke inside his trailer, so when he comes to see me, he knows he can't blow himself up just by having a Camel.

"Howard Johnson is clogging my cash flow. The Mexicans told me the whole story, if I'm translating right. They don't like buying from him. They can't understand what he's saying half the time. Goddamn language barriers in this country. This business," he says, letting a drift of smoke escape his mouth, "is becoming too ethnically diverse."

Lucky I got all the beers put down on the low shelf in the refrigerator. I can get to them when I'm bent over. I open a new one and don't even offer Lester anything. I tell him I don't know what he's talking about, and he says we are going to speak with Howard Johnson and it could get testy and I am his backup in case something goes awry.

Awry is Lester's word. I would never say something like that.

?

I have been in this bad cycle for months. Whenever Rhoda calls, it's always about money she's got to have. I have to work hard for my paycheck. I have to be able to haul a square of shingles up a ladder a few dozen times a day.

First, it was money for the gas bill that was high because she was awake all those nights trying to stay warm while she was throwing up. Then it was money for the doctor visit about the throwing up when she found out she was pregnant. Then it was money for the baby she found out about at the doctor visit. Everything in her life seems to be going in these big circles, but none of them steer her back in my direction.

I suppose I hoped the money I tossed out every once in a while would bring her home. Rhoda was not the kind to be out on her own. She didn't enjoy the possibilities of loneliness. Those damn hundred-dollar bread crumbs I kept leaving here and there, me thinking she'd follow them back to my porch because, I couldn't lie, I missed the woman. There was nothing like waking up in the middle of the night and being confused and thinking you were all alone, until she moved right next to you and you remembered all of the sudden that somebody wanted to be there, right there in that place with you.

But these days, I just wake up with nothing but space next to me. I open closets in the house and her smell pours out and it pisses me off. Not at her. We are never mean to each other. Rhoda isn't the mean kind. I just stay pissed off at the sadness of shit.

At least we aren't married. That would have cost even more money, more than I have. I asked her one time if that baby was mine. That was the only time she got really mad at me. "What do you think?" she said. And I told her thinking wasn't something I spent a lot of time on lately.

This morning, she'd said a hundred dollars would do her. "I need some vitamins. For the baby," she said.

"Hundred-dollar vitamins?" I asked her.

"These are special. For the baby," she said.

"I don't have a hundred dollars. I get paid on Tuesday. You got to get through the weekend," I said. She said that every day she waited on the vitamins was a risk I was making the baby take, said the doctor told her that.

"Come back home, Rhoda," I said, like I do every time she calls me up.

"I can't. It wouldn't be right. The timing ain't right. I need time. And I need vitamins." I could almost see her with the phone lodged between her shoulder and her jaw, twirling a piece of her blond hair with a couple of fingers. The only times I'd seen her since she left, her hair looked different. It was thicker and blonder.

I asked her about it, and she said that being pregnant brings on changes. I said, "No shit." But the longer she stays away from me the better looking she gets in my mind's eye. I suppose that's what always happens. If somebody isn't around, all you can do is fill in the blank spots.

"When you go to work today, see if they'll give you a little advance money. I can't work as many shifts now, with the baby. A hundred should be okay. I appreciate it."

I tell Lester I want to finish my beer and I will go with him, but it will cost him a hundred dollars. He raises one eyebrow. It surprises him because I never ask him for money. I don't ask because I get all paranoid that the DEA or somebody will trace Lester's twenty-dollar bills from some truck stop in Fayetteville through the Mexicans and right into my wallet. It's not like I'm saying I'm better than anybody else. I just don't want his meth money. But this way, going to see Howard Johnson and kind of being there, I figure I get an honest, easy hundred dollars. It isn't money for nothing.

Lester smiles. "Are you worth a hundred dollars, all bent over like that? Shit hits the fan, I need a stand-up guy, pardon the pun."

"Hand me another beer and open the truck door for me, goddammit," I say, pushing through the screen door, but I make sure I lock it behind me.

?

We call him Howard Johnson because we're lazy. We don't know how to pronounce his Indian name, so we settled on naming him after the old motel he bought and half-assed renovated. No telling how many more folks he's got living there. We never counted them up. I see children sometimes or an old woman at the Piggly Wiggly with the red dot on her forehead. But I've never been able to come up with a grand total. I just know they are here, and it doesn't look like they are moving on anytime soon.

The lot's got no lines, so Lester makes his own parking space way over in the corner, near the ditch at the road, a good fifty yards from the motel office. There isn't another car in the lot, but Lester won't take chances with his new truck. He loves that damn truck. It's a white Ford dually with glass packs and a trailer hitch. It can haul anything, but I have never seen a thing in the bed. There isn't a scratch on it. Lester waxes it once a week at night, under a couple of spotlights he put on the side of his house. Today he leaves it running, so I figure he thinks this won't take but a minute or two.

"I'll just wait here," I say. My back's loosened up some, but I really don't feel like standing up for long or walking across the lot.

"You can't give me the proper moral support from the cab of a pickup," he says back and reaches under the seat for his cut-down Louisville Slugger. He sawed a few inches off the barrel and sanded down the handle and produced a fine weapon of choice that fits under the seat of his pickup.

"You don't aim to hurt him, I know that," I say with more wishing in my words than I had planned on.

"I am an independent businessman in my crucial first year of existence, brother, and I am staving off a hostile takeover attempt at my core demographic. I don't necessarily aim for anything, but I am prepared for the worst. I have to keep food on my table for my family," which would have been a good thing to say if Lester actually had a family. He spends too much time cooking meth and watching Headline News and MoneyLine to have a family. "I am protecting the market share," he adds.

I ask Lester if I can finish the rest of my beer before we go and he says, fine, that will give him the opportunity to gird his loins, which I know is Lester-code for snorting up a head full of crystal. He ducks down in the seat. A breeze blows through the windows of the Ford, and I look in the direction of the wind. Thunderheads are building up behind the Howard Johnson's, and the leaves on the pin oaks are spinning a little in the air, but I think things may stay off in the west. I smell creosote or something in the parking lot. Maybe I smell Lester. Howard Johnson cut the grass this morning. I can smell that, too.

Lester sweats when he does meth, the way I do when I eat the hot salsa at the Dos Amigos restaurant. He reaches in the same place he keeps the Louisville Slugger, pulls out a beach towel, and wipes his forehead. The couple inches of beer in the bottom of my can are hot, but too much to waste.

"Let's go speak with the proprietor," and that's one of the things that gets me about Lester. There isn't any need to say anything, much less any need to use a word that big, but Lester spends most of his breath showing off these days. It's all a thing with him. He's okay until he opens his mouth and gives himself away.

?

Lester slaps the bell on the desk, and Howard Johnson walks in. Lester has the bat down at his side, behind his leg.

"A room?" he says, smiling and almost winking, looking at us like we're a couple, and this actually pisses me off. He knows who we are. He's seen us around. I know he's seen Lester's truck before. He's just baiting us. This is all beside the point. I can barely understand what he's saying. It makes me wonder how we're going to argue with him. He's shorter than I remembered, but he's squatty, like a linebacker. He narrows one eye the way Rhoda's cat used to do when it was bored.

"Room?" Lester says. "Yes, you could say that *room* is the topic of conversation this morning. You have moved into my room, metaphorically. I've spoken with our mutual Hispanic middlemen." He pauses. "I know, Mr. Johnson. I know all about it."

"A room?" he says again. "Lunch maybe?" He's got this blank look on his face, a deer frozen in headlights. I know he's playing stupid. I know that when I see it. He can speak English as good as I can. He's just trying to throw us off. Right then, I notice the meth bugs on the Indian's face. He must be snorting up some of his inventory. Those sores are a dead giveaway. I see Lester squeeze the handle of the bat. Sweat is beginning to roll down his forehead into his eyebrows.

Just then, a woman walks around the corner of the check-in place and stands off to the side. She's a good-looking, thin woman with chocolate-colored eyes and black hair that almost gives off its own light. And I happen to be where I can see Lester and this woman look at each other and that thing flies off between them, not that love-at-first-sight thing, but the other thing, that other look that says, *I already know you and I already had you and I want it again later when this is all over.* You know, that look. They aren't strangers, and they are way more than friends.

Right then, while I'm standing there, I feel things changing again. I wish I was up on a roof somewhere, watching the heat rise from a parking lot and hit the thunderclouds. You'd think Lester would have told me who he was banging and been proud of it. I'm not even sure when he had the time. Most nights I know of, Lester's cooking and watching for the wrong set of headlights to come down the driveway, but maybe if I think really hard about it, I've smelled curry floating in amongst the ammonia smells he brings over to my house when he wants a place to talk and smoke. Like I said, sometimes you wouldn't know we're even brothers. Brothers know about each other's women. That's almost a rule. And we're twins. That should count even more.

Funny thing or bad thing is, we all know now. Just because Howard Johnson speaks another language, he's no dumbass. No man is when his wife looks at another man like that. He sees the same glance I see, whatever you call it—a flick of the eye or a sideways look that hangs too long in one place.

"It's you?"

Howard Johnson says *you*, but he means a whole lot more than that, like Lester is the answer to a hundred questions Howard Johnson's had buzzing around in his head. Howard Johnson has his answer now. The woman stares down at her shoes.

I feel my back seizing up again, what with the beer wearing off and all this standing up I'm doing. I wish

I had one of those Indian beers I heard about. A Kingfisher beer. They are supposed to be good. I almost bought one in the fancy beer section at the Piggly Wiggly. Lester told me Kingfisher is the Budweiser of India, which is good enough for me. Now I know where he got his information.

"You didn't tell me about this woman thing," I say real low to Lester.

"I needed you to remain emotionally detached," he whispers back. Howard Johnson reaches toward the cash register and Lester slams the Louisville Slugger on top of the counter and that little woman jumps, but I swear Howard Johnson doesn't bat an eye, even the squinted one, when the wood cracks down. If Howard Johnson's doing crank, he's holding things together pretty good.

The two of them, Lester and Howard Johnson, stare at each other. The woman is shrinking as small as she can. I swear she looks tinier every time I glance over at her.

My back is starting to bend me over even more, and I have to go to the bathroom to get rid of some beer, so I feel the need to move things along and earn my vitamin money. "Look," I say, "Lester wants you to stop cooking up meth. That's why we're here. Just shut it down, Howard. You got plenty other things going on. Everything will be fine if you just shut it all down."

Lester and that woman cut their eyes at one another. This would be easier if it was just about the drugs.

This woman adds a bad wrinkle. I want to tell Howard Johnson that he could try moving his wife out to Terrapin Acres or Terrapin Place or whatever the hell it is.

"Stick to the motel business and everybody will be fine. Where is your bathroom? I got some rented beer I need to foreclose on." That sounds like something Lester would say. The shrinking woman nods toward the hallway. "I'll be back," I say to Lester and duck walk past all of them. Lester and Howard Johnson are staring each other down like a couple of dogs with a single bone between them. I don't want to leave them in the same room, but I don't want to wet myself in front of strangers.

When I find the bathroom door, I can barely push the damn thing in, my back is so stove up. I figure they have just cleaned the toilet, but while I'm bent there, trying to pee and keep from falling over, I notice that all the bleach and ammonia smell is coming from an air vent up behind me and not from the toilet, and the little bathroom fan is trying to suck it all up, but it can't keep up with the air coming through the vent. I try to pee and hold my breath, but that seems to work against itself.

Once I finish and somehow fix my pants, my curiosity is up. Just outside the bathroom there's another door that says *Employees Only*, so I limp on through it and head down this tiny hallway that smells like a janitor's closet, then through another door without a sign on it and into the room where I can tell he's been cooking up the stuff. The fumes and smell are so thick my eyes start watering. I holler out to see if anybody else is around and don't get no answer, which makes me think Howard Johnson and his wife have a family business amongst the two of them. Maybe those kids and the old woman are down in some of those rooms.

At that point, it's an easy thought that comes into my head. It's like somebody flipping a switch. It just all comes clear. I can earn my hundred dollars. I can make all Lester's problems go away. Hell, I might get a bonus. I'll buy vitamins for the whole damn year. Rhoda always said I never come up with ideas, that I just wait on somebody else's brain to fire. Well, I got me an idea now. It's just a matter of going back to the bathroom and turning off that piece-of-shit fan and stuffing some paper towels up in the air vent and then figuring out how to make some kind of fuse thing or another.

I limp back to the kitchen and find a dish towel. I shut the door behind me, letting all that smell and stuff build up a little more. Then I slide one end of the towel under the door as far as I can, then light the end I got in my hand. I blow on it a little so it glows and burns. The way I figure, eventually that ember will work its way under the door. I'm guessing I got a couple of minutes to grab Lester and haul ass, but by the time I get back to the little office, nobody's around. And I wasn't gone that long. It's not like I left them there for a half hour or something.

I check behind the counter to make sure the Indian isn't lying on the floor with a Louisville Slugger trademark on his forehead. I start counting off the time in my head when I hear a horn blow.

Outside, Lester sits in his truck, pulling on a cigarette and blowing smoke through the open window. Howard Johnson and his woman are standing in the middle of the parking lot like a painting, standing close. Nobody is smiling but nobody is bleeding. I walk as fast as I can across the parking lot. The wind has picked up again. As soon as Lester's smoke hits the air, it's blown away. But the rain is holding off. I could have put in a full day on the roof, a whole day of being above everything.

Even with the windows open, Lester has the air conditioning going. You can do wasteful things when you think you got money. I have to pull myself into the seat, my back hurts so bad. Lester hands me a big bottle of Kingfisher beer that's already sweating the label off. He's got it open for me.

"You got to move this truck pretty quick," I say.

"God bless us every one," he says, leaning back in his seat. "We negotiated a settlement. Howard Johnson gets the woman. I get my target market back. Everything is stable in the land. Love conquers all."

"I'm just saying, I earned my hundred dollars, maybe more," I tell him, and he isn't listening so I reach for the gear shift. "We need to leave."

"Whoa, now. Drink up, brother, and enjoy the breezes," he says, pushing at the knob on the vent and aiming it at my face. I look back toward the motel. Howard Johnson is still standing there on the asphalt, the edges of him wiggling a little in the heat. The woman is still finding her shoes interesting. Maybe the towel went out or something, I think. I take a sip of beer.

"A hundred dollars," I say.

"Well…" Lester stretches to show me how loose his own back is, I guess. "The way I see it, I really didn't need your services. When the deal was being struck, you were down the hall shaking hands with the Pope. Things could have gone south, and you wouldn't have been around. I handled it on my own. I figure a cold Kingfisher is payment enough for your efforts. We were only here ten minutes. You did not fulfill your end of the verbal contractual agreement."

I can't say anything for a second, first because it feels like somebody's got a screwdriver digging in my back, and second because I didn't think I heard right. "I got to buy vitamins for the baby," I say. "You don't understand."

"Just drink up. You'll be back on rooftops in no time." Lester sucks down another mouthful of smoke. "Look, here's a twenty for your trouble." He hands me a bill he already had in his hand. He's careful to flick his ashes way outside the window, so none of them blow back on the seats. Howard Johnson waves at us, trying, I suppose, to get us to move away from his parking lot. Behind him, the motel bakes in the sun. I hear a few cicadas buzzing, which means it's going to get even hotter, or it's going to rain, or both—I can't remember how that old story works. Howard Johnson pokes at the woman's shoulder, and I see him say something to her. She does as she's told and waves at us, just like her husband, but doesn't look up.

"I have never asked you for money before," I say.

"Brother, I am helping you by withholding funds. You don't need to be supporting that woman. I'm making you a man," he says. He's never liked Rhoda. He doesn't understand what it's like to have someone there when you come off the roof in the evenings. He doesn't understand how serious I am about things. His eyes are humming in his head, like he's had another taste of meth in the last few minutes.

I don't mean to spill my beer on the floorboard, but it works out for the best. Lester says, "goddammit" and reaches under his seat for the beach towel, which gives me a second to grab his baseball bat sitting on the console between us. Lester's busy dabbing at the beer in the carpet when I unfold from the truck, all bent over low toward the fenders.

I take out one of his headlights first with a single swing and hear Lester scream inside the cab. It doesn't seem fair, everybody getting what they need except me. Lester has his business with the Mexicans. Howard Johnson keeps his woman, but I end up eighty dollars short, and I got a back I can't hold up straight.

Another quick swing and I turn the other headlight into parts and pieces and start in on the windshield before Lester can get out of the cab and get close to me. He grabs my neck from behind, sticks his knee in my back, and tries to bend me straight. The pain blows out the top of my head. I can't think but to jam the end of the bat in his stomach. This stops him for a minute and gives me time to put some dents in the quarter panel.

I look at Howard Johnson for a split second. He is smiling and trying to get his wife to put her eyes on me. I wave at them and keep swinging. About the time Lester catches his breath and pulls himself off the pavement, the back end of the old Howard Johnson's goes off like a Roman candle, one big loud explosion that washes over us like a wave and knocks me flat on my backside. Shit begins falling from the sky. From where I'm lying on the asphalt, I smell the meth fumes blowing over the top of me, and my eyes begin to burn and water up in an instant. I can hear Howard Johnson, but I can't roll over to see where he ended up. Lester doesn't say a word. Just shakes his head, crawls into his truck, and puts it in gear, and for a second, I think he might run over me, but I know he just wants to get out before the fire truck or the sheriff show up. Lester doesn't like being caught out in the sun, especially when it's shining on trouble.

And I don't like being on the ground. All I can see from here are the clouds rolling in and the tops of a couple of trees. Thin smoke from the exploded motel moves just over my head. I can see what's left of a jet vapor trail breaking apart like spilled milk a mile in the sky. When I'm on the roof, the worst that ever happens is somebody puts a roofing nail through his thumb. Down here, people cook up things in their kitchens, and men pass looks to other men's women, and babies need vitamins.

I still have the bat in my hand. If I can get up from this hot asphalt and walk in the right direction, I will go home and pull my extension ladder out of the crawlspace under my house and climb up on my own roof. If I look far enough toward the clouds in the west, maybe I can see that place, that Terrapin Crossing, from where I stand, and I'll wave in the direction of Rhoda. I haven't swung a bat since Dixie Youth League thirty years ago, but it felt good to make some solid contact. I'll beat anyone who tries to get on my roof. I will figure out a way to get vitamins for that baby because Rhoda asked for them. I had a basketball coach in high school who always told us, "Boys, we're where we're at," and I'm no genius, but I don't know that you can ever be anywhere else than where you're at. And right now, I need to be somewhere else, somewhere above everything.

I hear sirens in the distance and a few, early raindrops smack the parking lot. I have to go now.

Acknowledgements

I'm grateful to the editors of the literary magazines who, through the years, noticed and published several of these stories. Many thanks to the ever-feisty Vine Leaves Press team, especially publisher Jessica Bell, publishing director Amie McCracken, and editor extraordinaire Melanie Faith. (I'm tempted to toss in a brand name here, just for you, Melanie.) Thanks to Jackson and Kat for countertop feedback in the home stretch. Thanks to Steve H., Janis L., and Hop R. for cheerleading from the Midlands. Thanks, as always, to Emily and Maggie for constant support. (Hey to Bean, Junie and Sof.) Thank you to Jack for continuing to ride the waves with amazing grace. Finally, thanks to Shannon, who always listens patiently, even when I ramble. Idiotically.

"Word of the Day" won the 2020 Larry Brown Short Story Award and first appeared in *Pithead Chapel*

"Playing Chicken" first appeared in *Pangyrus*, then later in the anthology, *Pangyrus 10*

"Taps on the Forehead" first appeared in *New Madrid Journal*

"What Gable Massey Did After his Wife Left Him," "Gable Massey Makes a Movie," and "The Prince" first appeared in *BULL*

"Smokey the Bear Has the Matches" first appeared in *Reckon Review*.

Also by Scott Gould

Things That Crash, Things That Fly
Strangers to Temptation
The Hammerhead Chronicles
Whereabouts

Vine Leaves Press

Enjoyed this book?
Go to *vineleavespress.com* to find more.
Subscribe to our newsletter:

Printed in the USA
CPSIA information can be obtained
at www.ICGtesting.com
LVHW032309021123
762954LV00049B/1175

9 783988 320308